NEW ALBANY-FLOYD COUNTY PUBLIC LIBRARY
33110003811153

ONE FOOT IN THE STIRRUP

Also by John D. Nesbitt in Large Print:

One-Eyed Cowboy Wild
Twin Rivers

ONE FOOT IN THE STIRRUP

John D. Nesbitt

Thorndike Press • Thorndike, Maine

Published in 1997 by arrangement with John D. Nesbitt

Thorndike Large Print ® Western Series.

The tree indicium is a trademark of Thorndike Press.

The text of this Large Print edition is unabridged.
Other aspects of the book may vary from the original edition.

Set in 16 pt. Plantin by Rick Gundberg.

Printed in the United States on permanent paper.

Library of Congress Cataloging in Publication Data

Nesbitt, John D.
One foot in the stirrup : western stories / by John D. Nesbitt.
p. cm.
ISBN 0-7862-1184-9 (lg. print : hc : alk. paper)
1. Cowboys — West (U.S.) — Social life and customs — Fiction. 2. Ranch life — West (U.S.) — Fiction. 3. Western stories. 4. Large type books. I. Title.
[PS3564.E76O53 1997]
813′.54—dc21 97-24788

for A.D. Nesbitt,
my first cowboy

Acknowledgments

"West of Dancing Rock" appeared in *Far West*, October 1978.

"To Quench a Thirst" appeared in *Short Story Digest*, Summer 1992.

"With a Shade of Grey" appeared in *Reader's Break*, 1995.

"Back from Bavispe" appeared in *Just PULP*, March 1981.

"If You've Got the Saddle" appeared in *Just PULP*, Winter 1979; reprinted in *Wyoming Rural Electric News*, April & May 1982.

"Spring Comes to the Widow" appeared in *New Trails*, ed. John Jakes and Martin H. Greenberg (NY: Doubleday, 1994).

To the editors of the above publications, I would like to express my appreciation for their recognizing and encouraging my work.

CONTENTS

WEST OF DANCING ROCK

Out on a spine of the first foothill ridge, a man could see how the town got its name. There, strung along the creek as it turned around the huge rock, lay the town in the shimmering heat that rose from the valley floor. Long before the town was there, men must have looked down and imagined the rock was dancing in the summer heat. Close to the top of that ridge I rested my horse and took the first stingy swallow of water — I was just into the foothills, and I had a whole mountain range to cross. In a dry year like this one, many of the old places might have nothing more than cracked mud. There would be a full moon, so I could travel some in the cool of night.

As I paused there looking back at the town, watching it over the hump of my canteen as I poured a trickle down my throat, there was a *thwang!* between my hand and my lips, and the canteen flew away. Then I heard the crash of the rifle. It sounded like a Winchester, but I didn't give a damn at that point what kind of a rifle it was. I kicked that buckskin into a run for the nearest clump of oaks. They were small oaks, low oaks, and that was what I wanted. Even a scrubby jack pine would do me right now, and those oaks looked like heaven.

A hundred yards from the oaks I had my second canteen slung over my shoulder, and the reins in my teeth. I was pulling my Winchester from the bucket as I felt a bullet slam into my horse. His whole body took the shock, and I felt it myself up to my shoulders. Down we went, with the rifle shot booming, and I was glad I'd shucked my rifle. I kicked free from the stirrups, spit out the reins, and, holding the gun up out of the dirt, rolled into a patch of manzanita. The horse rolled slam over onto the scabbard and didn't move, and I knew right then that I would never have gotten the rifle out in that position.

I lay still there for the longest time, maybe upwards of an hour or so, not even wanting to wiggle to better cover. Whoever it was couldn't see me now, and I wasn't about to give him a new target. So I lay there and waited, sweating, fighting off thirst, and wondering how good that water would taste when it was warm and brackish and my tongue felt as thick as a bedroll. Whoever it was, the sonofabitch was probably up there in the rimrock; so I judged from the way my canteen and my horse went. He probably had more shade, too, and the sun was just reaching its peak.

From where I lay the skyline was up and to the left, and the valley was down on the right. Since the two shots everything was deathly still and silent and dry and hazy. Way off to the right, wheeling in slow and patient circles above the valley floor, were the buzzards. Sometimes I saw four, and sometimes five. Tomorrow morning, or perhaps even late this afternoon, they would start on my horse. After that it would be something — or somebody — else. I gave in to a drink of water, sloshed it around my mouth and wetted my lips, and swallowed it with a gulp that I thought could be heard from the top of the ledge.

At some point I slept. For how long I don't know, but I awoke with a jerk. I was soaked with sweat, and sore; because of the sun, I figured it was after five. The first buzzard had landed on my horse. Maybe it was the flap of wings or the presence of another creature that woke me up. I scoured the rocks again, and again I saw nothing. Down on the valley floor I saw a wagon threading north. Two more buzzards landed on my horse, and I took advantage of the distraction to move into better shade. Again I studied the ledge, and I judged the distance to be a couple of hundred yards. Whoever the man was, he was a good shot, and he wanted me — or someone who looked like me — dead.

I had plenty of time to think, but in the next three hours till sundown I couldn't dredge a single name or face. Then, as the sun was slipping behind the mountains and the shadows were stretching down from the rim, a face from far out of the past loomed up in my memory. It had been six years earlier, a couple of months later in the year. I was riding the grub line, between outfits, when I rode down a quiet little draw. The autumn winds were getting nippy, and I had my right hand inside my sheepskin coat. When my horse's ears came up my hand came out, and I shucked my Winchester. Rifle across my saddle, I rode into a very unwelcome little scene.

What happened I was only able to put together later. One man was on his horse, keeping the rope taut on a steer's heels. A second man was leaning over a fire, heating up a branding iron, and the third man was just getting off his horse. I didn't like the lay of the land, and I didn't really care whose steer they were branding. Mostly, I just wished I'd ridden down a different draw, but it was too late for that now. The man sitting on his horse fired first, and I emptied his saddle. The one at the fire drew, and my shot spun him sprawled across the fire. The third man, half-dismounted as he was, re-mounted his horse and came straight at me. As fast as it all happened, I only had time to bring my rifle butt around and smash him in the mouth. That emptied his saddle, and I lit a shuck out of there. I heard a whole gang of shots, but I figured they were from the second man's gunbelt as he lay in the fire. I was sorry it had to happen, and I was sorry about that steer still there all hog-tied and helpless, but they didn't give me any chance. For months afterwards I could see that man's face as he raced head-on into my rifle butt, and I wondered if I would recognize that face again, busted up as it had to be. Now, lying in the manzanita out on that hillside, I was pretty damn sure that Busted Face would recognize me without fail. And from a distance.

How long had he followed me? Certainly not for long, or I would have known it. I always traveled alone, kept to cover, built no fires that could be seen, left no trail that was easy to follow, and stayed in no place long enough to be known well. Not that I was on the run — caution had just become a way of life, and out of second nature I always kept an eye on my backtrail. Now someone had gotten out on the trail ahead of me, and he had gotten me in his sights twice in less than a minute.

It has always struck me funny how a man can see something, register it, and think no more about it for years. Then at some unexpected moment the scene clicks, like the well-oiled cylinder of a six-shooter, and for the first time the scene makes sense. There was a man up there in the rocks who wanted to make buzzard meat of me, and there had been a man branding a steer six years earlier. Then there was the man in Wichita, only two years earlier, a man I'd never given a second thought to until right now. I had been dusting my hocks down the main drag of Wichita one August afternoon, thinking to cut the dust in my throat and toss away some of my wages at monte. I had the feeling of being watched, and as I glanced out to one side I saw a man standing behind a horse. Just as I looked, his hat lowered, and all I saw was the crown of a dusty sombrero and a pair of boots. The man was pulling on the saddle cinch on a *grulla* mare, and it seemed that he had pulled the mare sideways. But seeing no gun barrel resting over the saddle, I figured whatever the man was up to was his business.

I never saw his face that day, but I would have bet anything that evening on the hillside that below the dusty sombrero had been a busted-up face, and the same busted face had recently been squinting down the barrel of a Winchester at me. Now I had from sundown to sunup to think about that face and to wonder how many times it had looked on me. Had he first cut my trail in Wichita? in Laredo before that? or Denver? or Laramie? I knew I had a decent chance to slip down the foothills at dark and hoof it into Dancing Rock, maybe to ask around about Busted Face and make my way east back to Santa Fe. But he would always be there, either behind or ahead, and I would have no rest. No, here I would spend the night, and come daybreak I would see how the chips fell. I'd been rimrocked today, and I didn't feel like living every day of my life waiting for it to happen again.

The sun went down, and dark came. Then the stars came out and the moon rose. The moon, which I had earlier hoped to travel by, now lit up the hillside where I would spend the next several hours. I thought I would take advantage of the light, and move up and around the hillside. Even if he saw me, which was not very likely, he probably wouldn't waste ammunition, nor would he risk giving away his position. So I took my rifle and canteen, and as quietly as possible I picked my way through the brush and rocks. After about half an hour I was feeling loosened up and warm. The working of my muscles had burned off some of my tension, and I was relaxed but alert. Pausing to take a blow and get my bearings, I stood facing towards the spot where I expected my enemy to be holed up. I figured I was halfway around the hill and about a third of the way up. So I was most likely, from his point of view, up and away to the left from where my horse was.

As I was locating myself, I sensed something back down the hill from where I'd just come. I crouched behind a rock, held my breath, and silently laid my rifle barrel over the rock. About forty yards down the hill, a big buck stepped into my sight and paused. I couldn't count his antlers in the moonlight, but I could see he had a good-sized rack. His form was silhouetted in the silvery night, so I let my breath out and dropped him with one shot.

A shot like that, on a still, clear night in the mountains, is enough to make anybody sit up and wonder. I figured Busted Face was getting mighty curious, and I guess I smiled. Quickly I worked my way down the hill to the fallen buck, and I stood back as he kicked his last few kicks. I've always felt that a good clean neck shot spoils the least meat and messes up the least bones, but this time in the imperfect light I wanted a sure kill, so I had put one through the brisket. Besides, I had use for that trophy head. It had a large three-point rack, as I now saw.

Working swiftly, I gutted and trimmed the carcass. He was a good-sized buck for the foothills, and it took about all I had to get him hoisted. With a rawhide thong I tied his hocks together, stringing him up in a little oak tree that I reckoned was down the hill enough to be out of Busted Face's line of vision. I propped the cavity open with a small branch, to allow for cooling. Caping out the neck and shoulders, I cut off the head right behind the ears. With the head and cape of skin I worked my way halfway back to where my horse was, and there I laid my bait. Finding a cutbank about three feet tall, I chose a spot where there was a boulder just up the hill from the ledge. On the ledge there I built a foundation of small rocks and set the head solidly with the antlers sticking up. I laid the cape out and pegged it down with other small rocks, just for ballast.

With a grim smile I imagined my enemy scanning the hillside at sunrise. Down the hill, and a little to his left, he would see the antlers behind a rock. Many a hunter has had a blue jay point out a deer for him, and many another hunter has had a deer point out a man. And since deer usually prefer to stand behind cover and look downhill, Busted Face would figure that the deer might be watching me. He might also be interested in catching a look at the deer itself, seeing how big it was, or imagining how nice a target it would make. He might even wonder why it was still out feeding in the morning when there had been a full moon. Anyway, the sonofabitch had plenty to keep an eye on and think about.

Next I went back to my horse and got my rope, and then I started to climb up the hill on the other side from where I had first gone. Busted Face would be interested in the hill down on his left, and I wanted to be up and to his right.

When the sun rose over the mountains on the other side of the valley, I was cold and stiff. I had slept sitting up, with my toes against the trunk of a big manzanita bush and my back against a rock. The rifle barrel was cold, the dried deer blood on my hands felt cold, and the water in my canteen tasted cold. I held a mouthful for a long time, then spit it on my right hand. Wiping it clean on my shirt, I continued to work the hand. By the time the sun had cleared the far-off mountains, my hand was warm enough to do the work I had in mind for it.

The first landmark I picked out was Dancing Rock, cold and stark and still on the valley floor. Next I located my fallen horse, then the buck antlers. I searched where I expected my man to be, but I found nothing. I thought that maybe he had side-hilled in the night, and I doubted that it would have been to the left. Before long I saw what at first I took to be a deer, but it turned out to be a horse. A *grulla* horse. It was cropping grass almost directly below me. The hill fell away sharply from where I now sat, and it leveled out where the horse was. Just before it fell away again there was a clump of rocks, and that was where I figured my hunter had picked his stand. I kept my eye on those rocks, glancing away from time to time to see if the horse would point out the man for me.

By and by I heard a little rattling around in those rocks, and the horse perked up his ears. Suddenly a blanket and a saddle were thrown into a clearing in the rocks, so I figured my man had gotten up and was getting situated in his perch. There was a big rock right behind him blocking my view, but pretty soon I saw a boot stick out on the left side. For the longest time the boot sat there. Occasionally it looked like it twitched or moved, but I couldn't be sure. It did look, though, like he'd settled himself pretty comfortably for the morning hunt. I was tempted as all hell to shoot at his boot, and I sighted in on it a dozen times. But it was an awfully small target at fifty yards and downhill. I figured that if I waited, sooner or later something would bring him into my sights.

About an hour later, as I was starting to get mighty itchy and jumpy, a coyote came skulking down across the hill. He was heading straight for the buck antlers. I knew I couldn't run the bluff any longer, and all of a sudden I had me a hunch. The boot pulled out of view, and I knew that Busted Face was looking sharp downhill. So I threw my Winchester up to my shoulder and fired half a dozen quick shots down into that bunch of boulders. I hoped like hell for one lucky ricochet shot to give me the edge I needed, and I guess I got it. I saw both legs kick out beyond the rock, and then they both pulled back in. I sat back and considered. Now I had to go into that rattler's nest for a showdown. And the sooner the better, before he got to better cover. As long as I was up behind him I had the drop on him, and I had to work fast.

I tied my rope around the base of the manzanita bush, and I dropped the rest over the edge. It was a forty-foot rope, and the coils were stiff, so the end dangled about twenty or thirty feet from the little flat where his horse was. With the rope stretched out, I would have to drop only about twenty feet. If he didn't plug me while I hung there, I should have a good chance. I remembered how back home we used to tie a potato on a string and get it swinging from a tree branch for target practice. Bullets would knock little bits of potato all over hell. Now, as I leaned my Winchester against the rock, loosened the thong on my Colt, and started to let myself down hand over hand, I felt as helpless as one of those potatoes. But it was too far to jump all the way.

I had to start with my back to him, but as soon as I got over the edge I worked around so that my back was to the cliff and I was facing the nest of rocks. I went down quickly, burning my hands and straining my muscles. My feet were already below the end of the rope when he opened fire on me. Chips of rock and a spray of dirt bit into the back of my neck, and he was gone. I pushed off from the cliff with my feet, flung the rope aside, and hit the ground with a jolt. As I was coming to my feet he came around the other side of the rock, just as I expected, and it took him an instant to locate me. By then I had palmed my Colt, and at a distance of twenty yards I put a bullet through his chest. I stepped quickly to the left and sent another bullet through him. His flailing arms threw his rifle off to the side, and he crumpled to the ground. When I got over to him, his life was fading fast. He cursed me slowly, in half sounds.

"Gud . . . dim . . . yu' . . . dirt . . . ." Blood was frothing through his clenched teeth and strained lips. I must have hit a lung.

"Who the hell are you?" I demanded.

"Yu' . . . dirt . . . son . . . uv . . . bitch. . . ." And the last light flickered in his eyes. The grizzled features relaxed, and I recognized the same ugly face I had smashed that day with my rifle butt. His right cheekbone was lumpy, and his upper lip had been split and scarred into a snarl. Now it was all over, I told myself, and I didn't really even want to know his name. I would bury his body under rocks to keep the coyotes away. Any man deserved that. I would take only his horse, since that was all he had taken from me.

When I had buried him well, and gathered my rope and my rifle and my saddle and my venison, I rode the *grulla* mare back into Dancing Rock. That night, after I had traded most of the venison for jerky, cartridges, and a new canteen, I camped upstream from the town and roasted a hunk of venison for dinner. Tomorrow I would once again head west out of Dancing Rock and across the mountains.

TO QUENCH A THIRST

From the town of Alamogordo, Bradford Thorne dusted his hocks southward towards El Paso. The horse's gait was free and easy, and the man rode relaxed. An old Springfield carbine, tucked into a scabbard behind the saddle, was covered with an even coat of trail dust. The Colt on the rider's hip also had a fine layer of whitish dust, and it looked as if it hadn't been out of the holster in ages.

When the sun was high and hot, he rested his horse in the shade of an upthrust of rock. He rolled a cigarette and smoked it as he scanned the desert and his backtrail. There was no dust rising, only the glaring gyp flats and shimmering heat waves beneath a hazy sky. Anyone travelling this country in such weather had to have serious business, and it looked to Brad as if he was alone on the trail. No one had any reason to be following him anyway, but out of ingrained habit he watched behind him. Ahead of him, though, was a different matter, and from the point of view of Bradford Thorne it was serious. When he caught up with the party he was following, the dust was liable to come off those guns, pronto.

On the day previous, after two days on the range, Thorne had ridden home to an unexpected scene. The first thing he noticed missing was his dog. Usually on a hot afternoon Mesquite was lounging on the east side of the house or under the horse trough, and at the sound of hoofbeats he would come out to greet his master. But on this day no dog came. Looking around, Brad noticed that his other saddle horse, a chestnut gelding, was gone from the corral. Still looking around, he dismounted and entered the low-slung board ranch house.

The inside looked like a yearling steer had spent an afternoon there. The enamel water pitcher, the wash basin, tin plates, tin cups, and silverware were scattered all over the plank floor, interspersed with scattered dry beans and onions. Both bottles of whiskey were gone, as was the flour sack full of jerky. He knew before he went to his bedroom that the new Winchester would be gone, and it was. Then bewilderment set in as he imagined unknown, faceless men having free run of his house. It was the unknown that bothered him. Had some one done this out of personal spite, or had it been a random act of malice? Crossing through the main room on his way back outside, he noticed a deck of cards scattered on the table and several cigarette butts ground out on the floor. Had someone gotten tired of waiting for him?

Back outside in the hot dry afternoon, he realized he was thirsty. It seemed to him as he turned the crank that the bucket was heavier than usual. When finally the bucket cleared the foundation of adobe, it brought into view the soggy body of Mesquite, the dog. Deep in the pit of Brad's stomach something lurched. It was not nausea, but a jolt of dismay, anger, outrage . . . fear. Who was he up against?

After the first shock had subsided he noticed, with detached curiosity, an ugly hole through the dog's ribs. Whoever had done this had gone out of his way to cut Brad Thorne to the core. Within ten minutes of the time he finished burying Mesquite, he was packed and riding towards Alamogordo.

He had ridden on through the night after hearing that the chestnut was seen heading south. There were two men, as the tracks in his yard had told him, and in the Silver Rock Saloon he learned that they were down-at-the-heel-looking white men, most likely drifting trail bums. Brad wondered if they were luring him with such bold and careless action, or if they just flat didn't give a damn. At daybreak, horse and rider watered and then rested for a few hours.

Now at midday they were resting again. Thorne finished his cigarette and, grinding it out with his boot heel, thought of the cigarette butts in his house. He spat a fleck of tobacco from his lip, then took a sip of water from his canteen. When he caught up with the men who had ransacked his ranch, there would be hell to pay. He didn't care if he had to trail them all the way to Mexico. He was thirsty for revenge.

The sun was high on his right as he trotted his horse down the dusty main drag of Orogrande. The men he was following seemed in no hurry, so he thought it would be poor judgment to push hard in this weather — especially after men unknown to him. Leaving his horse and some terse Spanish directions with a Mexican stableboy, Thorne headed for the main cantina and eating house in Orogrande. He had been to the town several times during his ten years in the New Mexico Territory, and even though the Cerdo Bronco was no place to travel to for elegant cuisine, it modestly boasted the best beef, beans, and beer between Alamogordo and El Paso. The men he was following had probably stopped there, too, he reckoned.

The room was dusky and unlit when he stepped through the door, the only light coming from the afternoon glare outside. He stepped aside from the doorway, looked into a dark corner to adjust his eyes, and turned to the bar. He walked over and laid down a five-dollar gold piece. "Beef and beans," he said as the coin clinked, "and your coldest beer." The beer probably was the barkeep's coldest, but to Brad's palate it was only a few degrees cooler than the water in his canteen. After his first sip he looked around.

Down the bar there were half a dozen Mexican men, in the straw sombreros and cotton garb of the worker. They were chattering to one another and paid him no mind. Scanning the rest of the room, Brad saw only two dubious-looking cowpunchers, paunchy and drunk beyond danger, and two dusty, stubbled miners. The bartender, with the inevitable clipped mustache and slicked-down hair, brought him a steaming plate of beef and beans, plus a stack of tortillas wrapped in a towel. Then, as an afterthought, he brought the gringo a spoon.

"Do you go north or south today?" he asked, as if it were part of his duty to know the traffic flow of his town.

"South," said the cowboy, laying into his grub.

"Ees verry hot, eh *señor?*"

"Oh, yeah, hotter'n a two-dollar pistol out there," said Thorne. "This the coldest beer you got?"

"Coldest beer in Orogrande," answered the innkeeper, with an affirmative dip of the head.

"Yeah, I know." Then, resting his elbow on the bar and pointing the back of the spoon towards the barkeep, he asked, "You see two gringos ride through here ahead of me, maybe late last night or early today? One of 'em on a *caballo castaño?*"

The barkeep's eyes narrowed on his patron. "Are you the man that is called Thorne?"

"Yup," said Brad, returning the spoon to its original purpose.

"Your two *amigos* passed here yesterday at this hour, and sold one horse. Black one. They ride away on a *castaño* and a grey horse."

"They say anything interesting in here?"

"Maybe it is interesting to you, *Señor* Thorne," he said, drooping the corners of his mouth and shrugging his shoulders. "They said you can find your horse at the Gato Negro."

Brad stopped the spoonful halfway to his mouth, then shovelled in the grub. When he swallowed he asked, "Where's the Gato Negro?"

The host smiled. "In Juárez. Verry beautiful place, for *piojos* and *pulgas*."

From his change the cowboy pushed a dollar towards the barkeeper. "What's your name?"

"I am called Ramón by everyone in Orogrande."

"Well, Ramón, your message is interesting. Was there anything else?"

"Ah, yes. The one man he says the water is getting hot. You should understand."

"Hmm . . . can't say that I do right off hand. What did they look like?"

"One man, verry fat with *bigote*." The bartender stroked his own mustache as an aid in translation. "The other man, jellow hair and long."

The gringo pushed off his stool and picked up his remaining change. "Thanks, Ramón. I'll see you on the way back north. Always enjoy my meals here."

Back on the trail to El Paso he picked his teeth and mulled over the mystery. Who were these two unpleasant men with unpleasant intentions? And what did they mean that he was getting into hot water?

From the bartender's emphasis he gathered that the message had some double meaning. He wondered if he was to chase them all the way into the heart of Mexico, past Chihuahua and Durango to Aguascalientes. No, that was too far. They only needed to get him over the border, if that was their angle. Was there another clue? The water was getting hot. Had it been cool? His thoughts took an opposite direction. It seemed like some reference to his past . . . .

Before Alamogordo it had been Tajique, out of Albuquerque, and before that Tres Piedras. Drove the stage from Tres Piedras to Agua Fría. Agua Fría . . . and now it was getting hot? Had there been someone he had wronged back then, eight years ago? The job had been a tame one, from Tres Piedras through Taos to Agua Fría, and back again. There had been a couple of minor saloon brawls in Taos, but not in Agua Fría. Overnights there were usually pretty dull.

Then, like a pebble that for no reason is dislodged in a dry creek bed and tumbles and rattles down the slope till it comes to a new rest, a long-forgotten incident shook loose in his memory.

He had always kept a horse stabled in Taos, and once because of a schedule change he had ridden the horse to Agua Fría. Early one morning he went to the stable and found a stranger throwing a saddle blanket over his horse.

"I'll saddle my own horse," he had called out, and as he did so the stranger turned to draw. Not wishing to risk shooting the horse, Thorne put his first bullet through the man's right knee. Down went the would-be horse thief on his right elbow, and his gun was jarred loose. Bradford walked over to stand above the fallen man. "You're lucky," he said, "that I didn't want to put a bullet nearer my horse. Let's hope that sore knee keeps you off other men's horses from now on." The man crawled into a back stall to hide until Brad saddled and rode off; the incident lingered in his mind for a few days, but after that he thought no more about it.

The man had had straw-colored hair, he now recalled — that musty, dirty-looking color that some folks called dishwater blonde. As Thorne spat out a morsel of pulp from his toothpick he uttered a brief curse, wishing he had remembered sooner and had the presence of mind to ask if the man with the "jellow" hair walked with a limp. If the man did, then he was likely the one riding the chestnut.

The Gato Negro was, as Ramón had given it credit, a haven for lice and fleas. And, Thorne reflected, it probably housed some of the other exotic vermin, insect and human, that seemed to thrive in border towns. He saw no grey horse outside, nor did he see his own chestnut. Tying his horse to the rail and loosening the thong on his Colt, he drew a deep breath and pushed open the door. This was just the place, he thought, for them to do their work. Outside the pale of American law they could gun him down, and then return to the states and evade the jurisdiction of Juárez law.

Thorne tossed a dollar on the bar. *"Una cerveza,"* he said. The bartender brought a mug of beer, tepid to the taste. Here in the midst of this tawdry dive Thorne recalled the image of Mesquite, sodden and lifeless, and his stomach contracted as his anger boiled and welled up inside him. After his first sip, fighting the temptation to spit out the brew and fling the beer in the barkeep's face, he licked his lips and said, "Tell *Greñas* and *Gordo* that I came for my horse."

The other man, showing not the least surprise, called to a lackey from the kitchen. *"Ratoncito,"* he called, and when the lad arrived he lowered his voice. Brad caught the words *americanos* and *caballo,* but little else. Ratoncito scurried down a hallway that presumably led to the privy and other back alley commerce.

From that direction, Thorne presumed, would come one man, and through the front door would come the other. He decided to go first for the man from the alley, as the man at the front door would be an easier target and would have to adjust his eyesight.

A dull glow of light appeared and then disappeared from the hallway, and Thorne heard an uneven tread shuffle towards the barroom. The man paused before coming into sight.

"That you, Thorne?" a voice called.

"Yup," he called back.

At that instant the front door swung open to shed light on the crossfire, and Thorne lurched for the shadows. The flare of pistol fire lit up the end of the hallway, and Brad placed three quick shots at the spot. Then wheeling to his right he saw the looming figure of a large, heavy-set man in the doorway. He heard the roar of gunfire, felt his own pistol buck three more times in his hand, and then the room was quiet. As he reloaded his Colt he heard the bartender begin to sob and then chant in Spanish. He recognized the broken phrases as part of the rosary and realized that one of his opponents, probably the man in the hallway, had sent a stray bullet that way.

Thorne settled beneath a table and called out in the murky half-light. "Either of you saddle tramps want me, come after me." He expected another volley of gunfire, but all he heard was a shuffling sound, and then the bartender's voice.

"*Señor, Gordo* is dead."

"And *Greñas?*"

"I do not know."

"See if you can light a lamp," Thorne said. The barkeep produced a kerosene lamp, lit it, and set it on the end of the bar near the hallway. Brad walked quietly, out of the line of the man's fire, towards the gullet of darkness. At the side of the doorway he paused, where he heard a man gasping. It would be the straw-haired man.

"Throw out that six-gun," Thorne said, and a pistol clunked on the floor of the barroom. "Now crawl out here feet first," he ordered.

A pair of boots squirmed into view, then the legs and a bloody left thigh, then the elbows and hands of his unarmed enemy. Thorne stepped out into the open, and there in the dim light he looked upon the same face, twisted in pain, that he had seen on the stable floor in Agua Fría. Blood oozed through the man's fingers as he pressed against the wound on his thigh.

"You'll live," said Thorne. "I hope this time you learn to stay off another man's horse. That's both legs now, ain't it?"

"Yeh," said the man on the floor, and in that syllable Thorne comprehended a dozen curses.

"If you ever come around me or my place again," continued Thorne, pointing his pistol, "I'll be sure to shoot higher." He turned, kicked the man's pistol into the shadows, and started to walk away. As he was holstering his Colt he heard a scuffle behind him, and he turned around. The crippled man had reached back into the dark hallway and come up with a rifle. In the same instant that he recognized the rifle as his own Winchester, Thorne brought his pistol to bear upon the man and put a bullet through his jaw.

"*Damn* you," he said to the corpse, looking down at it. "I gave you two chances, and you wouldn't take 'em. I did what I could, and then I did what I had to." He picked up his rifle and turned to the bar.

"Barkeep!"

"Yes . . ."

"You tell Ratoncito to get my horse, the *caballo castaño,* and bring it around front."

The saloonkeeper sang out some orders that to Thorne's ear seemed appropriate.

Then the horse came around, and Thorne was in the saddle of the fresher horse. Riding the chestnut and leading the dun, he saw the gravel of the Río Grande fleet past beneath his stirrups. An hour north of El Paso he changed horses and rode on.

Back in the Cerdo Bronco he met the amused look of Ramón.

"And did the water get hot in the Gato Negro?"

"It damn sure did, Ramón, and I'd like to cool off with a drink of the coldest beer in Orogrande!"

WITH A SHADE OF GREY

My Winchester bucked at my shoulder and sent the tawny body rolling in the dust. My horse, good horse that he was, never flinched. When he felt me snake my rifle out of the scabbard, he just stood still and waited. I knew I had made a good hit, but just to make sure I rode over and looked at the body. A coyote was a coyote as far as I was concerned, and they were just about worth the lead it took to put them out of business. My father told me they followed the wagon trains out west, and now the hills and mountains were full of them. I didn't really know if they were natives or newcomers, but I did know they raised hell with fawns, lambs, and weak calves. So I did my good deed for the day. Since I was still a half day's ride from Corner Mountain, where I was to meet my brother, I wasn't too worried about the noise I'd made. Looking down at the coyote, I noticed it was a blend of yellow and grey. I usually thought of them as just yellow. I slid my rifle into the scabbard and kicked my horse into a trot. I thought to myself, there were quite a few people on this earth that made a living like that coyote.

Willow Creek flows and curves through the small upland valley at the foot of Corner Mountain. On the west side of the valley the land slopes down to the east, and on that slope there is an old apple orchard. That was where my brother had wired me to meet him. When I was a boy I used to shoot squirrels for Sam Crompton in that orchard. They were worthless ground squirrels — I got two cents a tail for bounty, and I used their bodies in my coyote traps. Between my shooting and my trapping, I earned my first rifle and my first horse.

Now, a good ten years later, Sam Crompton was in his grave and the apple orchard had gone all to hell. There were quite a few squirrels, too, and every time one would poke his head out of the ground, I would imagine blowing his head off for two cents. Thing was, you wanted to shoot him when he was away from his hole. Ground squirrels have it in them to get back in that hole, and cheat you out of two cents before they die. I sat in the shade of a pine tree, cleaning my guns and thinking how lucky those squirrels were. I went over to pick a couple of shriveled apples for my horse, and then I gathered up some firewood for the evening.

I had a good little bed of coals going and I was thinking about rustling up a pot of coffee, when my brother came riding up. His horse and his boots were still wet from fording the creek. "Light and set, Chad," I said. "Coffee's on the way."

Chad dismounted. He squatted facing me across the fire. He looked thicker, heavier, than he had when I'd seen him last. That had been four years ago. Maybe the business at hand made him look older and more serious.

"I thought maybe I'd lace it with a good runnin' shot of whiskey," I said.

Chad grinned, just like the same old Chad I'd always known. "Hell, you wanna ruin the whiskey. Save that coffee till the moon's high. I got some good cold spring water." He pushed himself up, walked over to his horse, leaned across it, and pulled up a soggy canteen. "I'd like to wash out the trail dust," he said. I dug out my two tin cups and my flask of bourbon, and in less than two minutes we were set up as pretty as any two dudes in Abilene.

I wondered who would bring up the subject first, and I guess I was just impatient. We raised our cups, clacked them together, and Chad said, "Here's how."

"Here's how," I said.

We both must have had a lot of dust to cut, because that first bourbon and branch didn't last long at all. When we raised up the second one, I said, "Here's to the old man."

Chad looked at me, his mouth grim and tight. "You damn right," he said. "Here's to the old man."

By and by Chad brought up the subject of supper. We'd been talking about the country we'd been through, the weather, the flies — all the no-account talk. I told him I had some jerky and some hardtack, which we could soften with some coffee. "Let's see what I got," he said. He walked back over to his horse, reached across to the far side again, and pulled up a bloody lump wrapped in a shirt. "Little old yearling fawn," he said, "had an accident."

Well, that was just like Chad, to ride up with the cold water and fresh venison on the off side of his horse. It was also just like him to sit there and leave his horse saddled, cinched, and bridled while he had a few drinks — and then maybe lecture me about shooting from off the back of my horse. He wasn't what you'd call ruthless, and he wasn't exactly considerate either. He just did things his way.

After the sun was down and the moon

was on its way up, we ate. When dinner consists of venison and whiskey and water, trail manners take over. We had juice running down our wrists and down our chins, and my tin cup was all smudged with fingerprints. We tossed some more wood on the fire. When my flask went dry, Chad brought out a full quart of whiskey. "Your horse must be pretty tired," I said, "carryin' all this stuff."

"He'll run lighter in the mornin'," Chad said. We never did get around to any coffee, but we knocked a hell of a dent in the whiskey supply.

Along about our fourth or sixth drink I must have started feeling brave. "How do you feel about seeing Ella again?" I asked.

"What you gettin' at?"

"I just asked a civil question. She *is* family, bein' the old man's wife."

"Didn't sound very damn civil."

"Aw, don't get a burr under your blanket."

"I'll put a burr under yours," he snapped, and straightaway he threw half a cup of whiskey and water in my face.

So there we were, swinging away at each other like it had been four days instead of four years. He got in the first good punch as I was coming to my feet, but I gave him one back in the jaw that let him know he still couldn't whip me, even if he was bigger. Then we were down and wrestling, each of us straining to stay on top as we rolled all over our gear. Finally we ended up with our legs locked, with my left arm beneath him and my right arm blocked. As he settled his right hand around my throat, with his left he grabbed a handful of my hair. Then he let go of my throat and started working on the left side of my face with short, powerful punches. At that point I said hell with it, and brought my left knee up into his groin.

That doubled him pretty well and relaxed his grip on my hair, so I broke free and rolled over and up into a crouch. Just for a second I saw him as my enemy rather than my brother, and I thought of kicking him in the face as he was coming to his knees. But I checked myself. "We're a fine pair," I said. "Here we come hundreds of miles to settle a score for the old man, and we got nothin' better to do than go at each other tooth and nail."

"Yeah," he said, wiping the blood from his nose, "we oughta save it."

It wasn't exactly the crack of dawn when we rolled out the next morning. Chad's face was sort of greyed, and his eyes looked like two holes burned in a horse blanket. I imagined I didn't look much better, especially with the saggy lump I felt on my left cheekbone. "Boy," I thought to myself, "he's still sore about Ella."

The two years' difference between us had been a lot back when we were growing up. After our mother had pulled her freight with the cattle buyer from Kansas, and the old man had gotten his fill of raving about what whores all women were, he'd brought home a fine-looking woman from Denver. "This is your new mother," he said, and that was it. With Ella around, he left off wondering out loud to us whether the sons of a whore would ever come to anything. That is, until it came out that there was something between Chad and Ella. That was where the two years mattered. I was fifteen and still wondering what it would be like, while Chad was seventeen and not telling me anything.

Chad left first, but I wasn't too much longer for the home place. I got tired of being the second son of a whore, and always getting those looks that said, "So you'll be trying it next." But rather than follow Chad to Wyoming, I went to Arizona. In the next eight years I heard nothing from home, and I heard from Chad very rarely. During that time I saw him twice — once when I rode up to Laramie, and once when we were both in Denver — but we didn't talk much about the family either time. We talked a lot about cows, and some about horses. But from a word dropped here and there, I gathered that he kept in touch.

"Well," I said, as the coffee grounds were settling, "what's it look like?" The telegram had said only that the old man was dead and that we would meet here.

"Shot right out of the saddle, on his own property."

"Any clues?"

"Henry .44, looked like."

"Any hunches?" I poured the coffee.

"Yup. A couple of jaspers."

Jaspers. That one word brought back to mind a clear and distant memory, as I'm sure Chad meant it to. The incident had taken place about fifteen years before, when Chad was about ten and I was about eight. It was a warm, moonlit night in July, and we were riding back from town with our father in the buckboard. Chad and I had spent the day playing with other boys in town and snooping through all the barns and stables. The old man, who wasn't all that old at the time, had bought the regular supplies and had settled down to a few hours of poker. When he went to town he liked to be seen as a gentleman, and he wore his nice black Stetson and his black frock coat. He never packed a pistol, but he did carry a rifle in the buckboard. Well, we knew that when he sat down to have a polite drink and play a polite hand of cards, we weren't to bother him. He came out about sundown, walking fairly straight, and we went home. All the way home he didn't say much, except every once in a while he'd mutter something off-hand, like "Sonofabitch drew three cards and hit a full house," or "Purebred Morgans my ass."

Chad and I were surprised when we stopped about a quarter of a mile from the house. We could see a dim light in the window. The old man lifted the rifle from in back of the seat and said, "You boys wait here. I'm going ahead to look things over." He'd braced himself pretty well in no time, and the liquor wasn't bothering him a bit. We waited till he got to the house, and then we went on down ourselves to get a peek. It being July and the window open, we could see and hear just fine.

There were two rough, ugly-looking men sitting on chairs in the living room. One had a rifle across his lap and the other had a shotgun. They were facing the front door. Suddenly the door behind them opened — the old man must have come slow and quiet down the hallway from the back door. "Didn't expect company," he announced. Both men jerked around, only to see that he had the drop on them. "I'd offer you a drink," he said, "but I see you've already helped yourselves. Sorry you can't spend the night."

"See here, Hollister," said one of the men, "we only came to talk about the grazin'."

"Talk's over," said the old man. "You two jaspers fork your broncs and get the hell out of here. And when you pass my buckboard, don't so much as look at my two little boys or I'll ventilate both your ugly heads. I'll be right behind you."

All the rest of the time we were growing up, the word "jasper" had been a secret and thrilling word between us. I remember first wondering, at that point, if my father had ever killed a man. And now, as I watched Chad spinning the cylinder on his six-shooter, I wondered if my brother ever had.

"Huh," I said, taking up the conversation again. "Why do you think Carbeau and Slattery would want to kill him? I thought all that business was done long ago."

"Part of it," said Chad, drawing a breath, "was for the range. The old man never filed legal claim to it. And the other part of it —" Chad hesitated and went on, "Ella thinks they were cuttin' the old man's herd. You know how he was, casual about brandin' his stock, careless about where it grazed."

That was the old man, for sure. Always preferred not to know exactly how much he had, so long as he could always round up enough two- and three-year-olds for what he wanted to sell. Thought it was small-minded and un-gentlemanly for a man to fence the range and brand all the cattle he could slap an iron on. I can't say that Chad or I either one felt the same, but that didn't matter right now. The old man had been drygulched, and Chad had a good idea who had done it. Loren Carbeau and Emmett Slattery loomed uglier than ever in my mind. Jaspers.

"Where do you reckon they are?" I asked.

"They still got that beggarly cabin up on their spread on the Jalama, but right now they've got a work camp right where the southern slope of their spread meets the old man's."

"Then you didn't just get here."

"Hell, no," he said. "I been here a week lookin' around. I wired you from town." He shook his coffee grounds into the fire, picked up a big pine cone, and walked towards the creek.

"They got a brandin' camp?" I asked.

"Sure as hell ain't buildin' a school house," he said. He flung the pine cone into the creek, and as it hit the water he palmed his Colt. With three of the six shots he chipped and splintered the cone, and the other three kicked up water right around it. Chad had gotten pretty good.

"Practicin' for them?"

"Naw," he said, "I got a varmint duster for them." He holstered his hog leg and went over and picked through his gear. I had just seen the stock before, figuring it was a saddle gun, but now he pulled out a shiny double-barrelled shotgun. It looked deadly.

"Two barrels, two jaspers," I said. "Comes out even. You invite me along for the company?"

"You never know," he said, and to tell the truth, I didn't know. "Thought we'd ride over and talk to 'em today," he added.

I thought to myself, no need to waste any time.

They were just letting a calf up from the branding when we rode into their camp. They looked quite a bit as I remembered, only not so ugly. They were ugly — dirty from their work, and jowly — but not the monsters I remembered. Carbeau spoke first.

"Howdy, strangers. What can I do for you?"

"Name's Chad Hollister," my brother said. "This here's my brother Henry." Both men looked from Chad to me, and I just nodded, hands on my saddle horn. There was a moment of silence, then Slattery spoke.

"Heard about your pa. Hell of a thing. . . ."

"I bet you heard," Chad cut in.

"What d'you mean by that?" Slattery snapped back.

Chad pulled out that deathly shotgun, and it made my flesh crawl. "I bet you saw some, too," he taunted.

"You got no call to talk to me like that," Slattery said, with a quiver in his voice.

Chad was getting ugly. "I'll talk to you any way I want, you snivellin' sonofabitch." He swung his shotgun around, and Carbeau clawed for his gun. Chad dumped him with the first barrel, and swung around to Slattery. The blast of the second barrel tore at Slattery's left arm, but he came up with his pistol.

"Now is where I come in," I thought, with my pistol pulled. I aimed at Emmett Slattery, squeezed the trigger, and killed my first man. Chad looked around at me as I slipped my six-gun back into the holster.

"Told you you never know," he said, and I still didn't.

Back on the trail to Alamosa we came to a crossroads. We turned our horses facing each other and we shook hands. I had already mentioned that I didn't want to go back to the old place. At that moment I didn't want anything except to be alone. I had a catch in the back of my throat, and my stomach felt like there was a lump of cold steel in it. The lines and colors were blurred in this business, as if Chad had drifted grey dust over it all. It was nothing I could brush out clear at the moment, so I just said I had to get back to my own place.

"Pay my respects to the old man," I said. I didn't mention Ella.

"Will do," he answered, reining his horse around.

"Chad?"

"Yeah, Henry?"

"You sure they done it?"

"Good enough for me," he said, and with that he kicked his horse in the direction of the home place and everything the old man had left behind.

BACK FROM BAVISPE

The lurching and swaying motion of the stagecoach brought Hagborn to consciousness. With some effort he opened his eyes, trying to remember where he was and where he was going. Dust was thick inside the darkened coach, and the smell of human sweat hung heavy in the air. In the dim light he could make out the slumped form of a man in uniform, seated across from him. As Hagborn went to push himself upright he noticed, to his dismay, that his hands were cuffed together. In order to sit up straight, he had to push on the floor with his heels and scoot with his haunches. The small commotion awoke the soldier in the opposite seat.

"Well, gringo, you are finally awake. How is your head?"

Jim Hagborn, or Hag, as his trail pards called him, then realized that the soldier's uniform was the greenish-brown issue of the Mexican army. And the carbine leaning against the soldier's leg, like the handcuffs on his own wrists, had the purpose of keeping him in the coach.

"My head hurts like hell, amigo. Where are we going?"

"To Durango, gringo. And when we get there, you will not think I am your *amigo*. I am no friend of the man who keels Don Bernardo Zendejas."

"Who killed who?"

"Everybody in Durango knows that three gringos shot to hell Don Bernardo in his hacienda and esteal his horses, and run for the border. You were estupid to remain in Agua Prieta."

Agua Prieta. That was where the headache came from. Hagborn tested his head with a shake, and a sharp pain shot from his right temple to his left jaw. His whole head felt swollen and itchy inside, and he could feel the saggy swell of a bruise on his right cheekbone. The soldier, and maybe some of his friends, must have done some boot polishing on Hag's head and ribs. The last thing he remembered was dancing on a table top in a border town cantina. He and some fellow cowhands had spent a few days in Nogales and had drifted down to Douglas and across the border to Agua Prieta. It was a small border town, but there were supposed to be good times there. Well, he guessed he'd had that. There had been tequila, and a well-rounded girl named . . .

Esperanza? Some of the headache must be from the tequila, but at this point it didn't matter. The girl, Esperanza, was gone, as was the tequila. He was in a stagecoach on his way to Durango, and he didn't have to ask whether it was the Durango in Mexico or the one in Colorado.

"And you think I'm one of the killers?"

"You are gringo, no? And you ride a palomino horse? And you wear a red *camisa?* You are barely dead already."

"You fellas jump pretty fast. You take a man coming south to spend his wages and you tell him he's a killer running north, because he wears a red shirt. The Mexican army doesn't have enough handcuffs for every cowboy in Arizona that wears a red shirt."

"Don't worry too much, gringo. You are going to see Don Bernardo's daughter, and she is more pretty than the one you dance with last night."

"His daughter?"

"*Sí.* She promises to pay ten thousand pesos to the man who brings back the man who keel her father."

Hagborn had always had a special interest in pretty señoritas, but right now he had no desire to meet Don Bernardo's daughter if it was just to see the fire in her eyes as she paid for the privilege of watching him die.

His own eyesight was improving now, and he could see the swarthy face of the sergeant. The face was shiny, and gold-lined teeth flashed out of a wolfish leer. His right hand moved to the carbine, and he leveled it at Hagborn's lap. Earing back the hammer, he pushed the muzzle of the rifle into the front of Hag's pants. "You will like her, gringo. She is beautiful, and verry, verry beautiful when she is angry." He jabbed a couple of times, and then laid the gun across his lap, hammer still back.

Although his hands were cuffed, Hag was able to fish out the makings and roll himself a cigarette. The sergeant shot a glance at the tobacco. "Eef you let me make a *cigarro,*" he said, "maybe I will let you drink at the next estation." Hag handed the little cloth bag to the sergeant and watched him roll a smoke. The flame of the match lit up the Mexican's face like a fire against a rock wall. The man exhaled, then grinned. "Eet is lucky you don't smoke cheap tobacco, or you drink out of the horse water." He laughed at his own joke, and so ended their conversation.

For what seemed like endless hours, Hagborn sat and rocked in his seat. From the turning and leaning of the coach he imagined that they were climbing the steep, winding southern trails into the Sierra Madre. With his back to the horses, to the south, he was getting queasy in the stomach; however, he knew better than to change seats. Whenever his eyes met the other man's he saw contempt and disdain. He was sparing with his smokes, also, because he knew it would cost him two cigarettes each time — and the sergeant rolled himself a generous quirly. Finally the creaking and jostling came to a halt, and the door swung open. The light burned at Hag's eyes, but he was glad of the chance to stand on solid ground and stretch his legs.

The sergeant strutted to the little hut, shouting a two-syllable command louder and louder. After a long moment a dried old woman emerged from the goats and the flies and the chickens. She gummed out a greeting.

"*¡Agua!*" commanded the sergeant, suddenly a general in posture and voice.

The old woman moved to a circle of rocks beneath a lean-to, removed some boards that served as a cover, and hauled up a wooden bucket of water. The sergeant commandeered a gourd dipper hanging from a rafter and helped himself to several ladles of water, most of which he successfully poured down his gullet. When he had drunk his fill, he tossed the gourd into the wooden bucket and walked to the far corner of the open lean-to. There he paused, dabbing his brow and face with the cuff of his dusty shirt.

Hagborn was still trying to imagine how he would handle the dipper with handcuffs when the old woman walked up to him with the gourd and bucket. Raising the dipper above her own head to meet his mouth, she served him a drink. Then she helped him with two more, making a much neater job of the act than the sergeant himself had done. When Hagborn's thirst was quenched, he looked at the woman and nodded. In eyes that to the sergeant were as dull and blank as stones, Hag saw compassion and sympathy. In that instant he realized, from her look, that she pitied his present condition and pitied even more deeply what lay in store for him.

When the horses had been watered, and when the sergeant had sniffed out a cooked haunch of goat for himself, he beckoned to Hagborn to crawl back into the coach. With an imperious jerk of the head he barked, "To Durango!" Hag crawled in, not without effort, and sat back on the bench. His guard sat down opposite again, with the rifle across his lap. As the coach groaned its way back onto the desert, the sergeant went to work on the roast. Amid the creaking of the stage Hag heard sounds of appreciation as the other man cleaned the haunch right down to the bone.

It seemed that Hag had just fallen asleep again when he was startled by an object hitting his bench. Looking down to his right, he saw the haunch bone. "Go eat dinner, gringo," said his escort. "I do not have a dog at my house." Then he eared back the hammer of his carbine again and leveled the muzzle towards Hagborn's belt. "Gringo, what do you theenk if I . . ." By now Hag's patience had run out, and with no hesitation he kicked the rifle upwards. The rifle fired, sending a bullet through the roof. Hag heard a scream, no doubt from the driver, and the horses bolted. Closing in on the sergeant before he could lever in another shell, Hag knocked him backwards with both fists together. The handcuffs gave Hag just enough freedom to get both hands around his enemy's throat. The man thrashed and flailed, but the fight for life was stronger in the upper man, who focused all his will and strength down through his arms to his hands. Presently the flesh relaxed between his thumbs and fingers, and Hagborn returned his thoughts to the situation around him.

The horses were running faster and faster now, and the coach was clearly out of control. It was careening from one side to another, groaning and screeching. The driver must be a mile back, eyes wide to the sun, and Hag had no desire to ride this one out to the end of the line. Kicking open the door of the coach, he saw the mountainous desert bouncing and jerking past him. He perched on the ledge of the doorway, took a deep breath, and pushed off with his legs. He took the fall with the length of his left side, as he planned, but the impact knocked his wind and his senses out of him. There was one fleeting image of him rolling, rolling, in the direction of the stagecoach towards Durango. Then he came to a stop at the base of a saguaro cactus, and there was nothing more.

When he awoke he did not know if it was late evening or early morning. The sun was pink in the distance, but he did not know if it was east or west. The air was cooler now. Some animal was licking his face where the sweat ran. Suddenly his tobacco sack slipped out of his shirt pocket, and his damp face was flecked with tobacco. When he got his eyes cleaned out, he found himself looking into the bulging eyes of a grey-black billy goat. The string and top of the tobacco sack hung out one side of the goat's mouth, and the goat's jaws worked sideways back and forth on the new-found delicacy. As Hagborn's eyes began to focus, he saw a wizened little old blister of a man standing behind the goat. He wasn't much bigger than the old woman, but instead of a dipper he had a rifle.

"Welcome to Bavispe," he said.

"Where the hell is Baw-vee-spay?" asked Hagborn, rubbing the rest of the tobacco grains from his face.

"We are in Sonora. The Río Bavispe is over there." The old man motioned over his right shoulder with the carbine. "Bavispe is a *pueblo*."

"Where is Durango?"

"Oh, too far. Over there." The old man pointed straight to his right. "Maybe ten days with a horse. Too much for you in cowboy-boots." The old man squinted at him. "Why do you love to walk to Durango?"

"I got no love for Durango. Some greasy sergeant was taking me there." Hag held out his handcuffs, as if to leave no further question.

"Ahhh!" said the old man. "The *federales* had you."

"Who the hell are the Feather Alleys?"

"They are the *soldados* for the *presidente*. Carrancistas. For Carranza."

"I sure can't keep up with your presidents. One day it's Diaz, another day it's Huerta. I even heard that Pancho Villa was."

"One time he sat in the chair, they say, with Emiliano Zapata on one side. But now it is Carranza, and he and Pancho Villa are like thees to each one!" He made an unmistakable gesture with his finger across his throat, to summarize the Carranza-Villa rivalry. Then he asked, "Why do you go to Durango?"

"This sergeant, or whoever he was, said he was bringing me back for killing some Don Bernardo. I never been there before."

"We hear a little of the story. The men who kill Don Bernardo were *gueros, muy blancos*. They have yellow hair. You, you are *moreno,* dark enough to look like Mexican. That sergeant, he wants to sell you."

"Ten thousand pesos."

"That sergeant," said the old man, with a wise and slow shake of the head, "ees no Carrancista in his heart. He is *coyote*."

"You mean a bounty hunter?"

"We call him *coyote*. Many of them used

to be the *rurales,* the old police. They carry the uniform of the *federales,* but they do not fight for Carranza. They esteal for themselves. Like the *rurales,* they take my goats and my sheep. And they sell gringos."

"Well, there's one of 'em out of business," drawled Hagborn. Then, in a mixture of cow country Spanish and unnecessarily broken English, along with clumsy gesticulations with his handcuffed hands, he told the details of being shanghaied out of Agua Prieta. With some hesitation he told how he had throttled the sergeant, and then his story ended. To his confusion, the old man swung the carbine around and ordered Hagborn curtly.

"Put your hands high over your head." Hag raised his hands, wondering what part of his story had disagreed with the old desert rat. Suddenly the old man raised his gun and fired. Hag felt his hands pull backward, over his head, and then apart. The bullet had cut the handcuff chain in two. "We will finish at my house. Come, *hijo. Ven, Chapulín.*" The billy goat, which all this time had been reclined in the shade of Hagborn's cactus, pushed himself up on his feet and trotted out in front of the old man and his guest. The three of them headed in the direction of the Río Bavispe.

Near the close of the evening — and evening it turned out to be — they stopped at a squalid hut, little more than a stack of sticks. In his hunger, Hagborn fancied that the hut would make a nice fire over which to barbecue Chapulín. Hag thought it only fair that since he had fed the goat, the goat might now feed him. But to his surprise the old man emerged from the hut with a bundle wrapped in cloth. *"Costillas de borrego,"* he said, putting his fingers and his thumb all together and pointing at his open mouth to symbolize that dinner was on its way. The bundle turned out to be ribs, with too much fat on them to be goat. When his host got the ribs to sizzling over a small fire, the gringo recognized the odor of broiled lamb and remembered the meaning of *borrego*.

Hagborn left his best Nogales and Tucson manners behind when the meat came off the fire. The two men ate without talking. When the old man threw a couple of small faggots on the coals, the flames lit up the grease around his mouth. Hag imagined his own face to be at least as shiny. "Well, amigo, that was pretty damn good," he said. Hag threw the last rib bone in the fire, amused at his repeated impulse to throw the bones to their fireside pet. With each bone he realized that Chapulín, act as he might, was not a dog. After a brief pause and reflection, Hagborn spoke again to his host. "Now that you've saved me from the coyotes and the buzzards, and given me some first-rate barbecued lamb, can I ask you your name?"

"My name is Miguel Bonifacio Vásquez de Hinojosa," he said, with graceful cadence, "but everyone calls me Tío Boni." With his cotton sleeve he wiped the grease from his mouth, and smiled at Hag. "You call me *Tío,* too. It means onkel. And you, how are you called?"

"My name's Jim Hagborn, if you can get your tongue around it."

"Yeem. Yeem Hcag . . . maybe better I call you Diego. It means Yeemee."

"That's fine by me, Tío. I'll be Diego as long as I'm in Sonora."

"Also," added Tío Boni, his eyes twinkling in the firelight, "we get you better clothes for the desert. I will change you a *sarape,* some white *pantalones,* and *huaraches,* for your red *camisa,* your *chaparejos,* and your cowboy-boots. We sleep here at the *ramada* for when the moon is high, and we go to my house." Without further ceremony the old man stretched out by the fire and closed his eyes. Hagborn pulled off his conspicuous boots, placed them so that the shanks overlapped for a pillow, and closed his own eyes.

The moon was high and bright when Hag awoke. The old man was rustling around in the hut. He came out, rifle in hand. *"Vámonos, Diego,"* he said, and *"ándale, Chapulín."*

"What's his name in English?" Hagborn asked.

"Chapulín? He is the *saltamonte,* you know, the *insecto* that —" Here the old man paused and, putting his ankles together, did a quick little hop in the moonlight.

"Jumps? Grasshopper?"

"*¡Eso es!* Chapulín yomp like no other goat."

"And you. You never told me if you side with Carranza or Villa or whoever."

"Well, we are in Sonora, so we like Obregón. He is Carrancista. But Pancho Villa, he pays me money for my goats and sheep. Carranza sometimes, too. But the revolution is not good for the *campesinos,* the *peones.* I want to sell my sheep in Arizona before the *federales* esteal them."

"They just come an' take em, eh?"

"They ride on their horses, and shoot what they want, and tell me to skinny it. Better I sell to the gringos. They always pay me, but the *federales* just sometimes."

In the moonlight, Hagborn followed the old man and the goat along a trail that led westward through scrubby oak mountains. After about three ridges, and perhaps a couple of hours of hard walking, the old man halted them at a ridge top. Below them lay a mountain valley. "Bavispe," he said, pointing to a small twinkle of lights to the north. *"Mi ranchito,"* he said, gesturing to the left, "over there." And then, waving his hand from left to right, he pointed out a small grey ribbon that sparkled along the valley. *"El Río Bavispe."* The gringo exhaled heavily, relieved and grateful that only a few downhill miles remained for the day's travel.

Tío Boni's house was dark and quiet when they arrived. The old man showed the cowboy to a low, dark stable, where Hagborn understood he was to finish his night's sleep. When morning came, Hagborn was nudged awake by the old man. "Come to my house," he said. Hag pulled on his boots and followed his host to the adobe building.

Entering the kitchen, he saw two women with their backs to the doorway as they worked at the stove. The women turned, and Tío pointed to the nearest one. "My gwife," he said. The woman appeared somewhat younger than her husband, but well into middle age. Her hair, still thoroughly black, was combed back from a finely featured face that was lined from years of work in the sun.

"Mucho gusto," she said shyly, wiping her hands on her apron. Hagborn nodded.

Tío then pointed to the second woman, an older woman who reminded Hag of the woman at the way station. "My mother," said Tío; "she is called *Abuelita.*"

"Mucho gusto," she said, with an ancient voice.

Hagborn nodded and managed to say, in flat cowboy tones, *"Mucho gusto."* Tío then pointed to a chair at the table, and the gringo sat down.

In a matter of seconds there was a steaming plate of frijoles in front of him, with a stack of tortillas wrapped in a cloth in the middle of the table. Just as he was finishing his second serving and was sopping up the remaining juice with a tortilla, the blanket moved in the doorway. He flinched, unaware that there might be anyone else in the house, and fearing the entry of the *federales* or other agents of the law. His fear quickly gave way to surprise when the opened doorway revealed a señorita — a young woman dressed as modestly as the rest of the family, but whose clothes could not conceal that she was fully arrived to womanhood. Hagborn's heart thumped and his stomach fluttered as the girl spoke.

"Buenos días, papá. Mamá. Abuelita."

"Diego," said the father, "thees my daughter, Petra. *Petra, éste es un amigo americano.*"

The young lady smiled and nodded, much in the manner of her mother. Hagborn lurched to his feet, desperate for some act of chivalry and conscious of the cuffs that were still on his wrists.

"Mucho . . . mucho gusto," he stammered.

"Mucho gusto, señor," she rippled back as she sat down.

For the first time Hagborn realized that his Spanish vocabulary was limited to livestock, landscape, and food. Hoping to make a good impression on the family in general, he turned to the two women at the stove and said, *"Buenos días"* as gallantly as he could, and walked outside into the sunny morning.

In a very short while he had formed a whole new idea of the Mexican people. Not all Mexicans, he reflected, were border town whores or desert cutthroats. For every brigand like the sergeant, there must be a dozen warm-souled folks like Tío Boni and the old woman at the way station. Hagborn rebuked himself for wishing that, on top of all of the old man's hospitality, he might have a little tobacco. After such a warm and filling breakfast, he felt the itch for a smoke.

The gringo was casting glances around the farmyard to see where Chapulín might be, when Tío Boni emerged from the house. He motioned to Hagborn to follow him back inside.

Hagborn emerged the second time looking for all the world like a Mexican *campesino.* In very little time he had replaced his red cowboy shirt, striped pants, leather chaps, and cowboy boots for the drab white peasant shirt and pants and a pair of leather-thonged sandals. With his sun-burned face and wavy dark hair and mustache, he felt less conspicuous than he did tromping through the Sierra Madre in a red shirt and cowboy boots.

Just as he was wondering how long it would take to get a sun tan on his feet, he saw Tío come out of the house again.

Producing a little goatskin bag tied by a thong, the old man asked, "*¿Cigarro?* No smoke, no *mexicano,* they say."

Hagborn took the bag, rolled a quirly, and returned the makings to Tío. "Thanks," he said.

The old man rolled himself a thin little smoke — unlike the sergeant, Hagborn thought — and handed the bag back to his guest. "For you," he said. "Chapulín no eat thees one."

During the middle part of the morning, after hacking off the handcuffs, Tío showed Hagborn his ranchito. Hag learned that the two men would drive about forty head of fat lambs to Douglas, Arizona, where the U. S. Army would buy the stock and distribute it among the Indian reservations and the Army posts.

In the course of preparations for the trip, Hagborn was introduced to the pack burro they would use. The gringo couldn't remember ever seeing a less agreeable animal — the size of a pony, the color of a rat, and the smell of a goat — but he was glad to have a beast of burden.

"Guanga," said the old man.

"Guanga? Her name?"

"Yes."

"What's it mean?"

"Many years. Old one."

When Hagborn asked if they three would be the party, Tío replied that Chapulín would go along, too. All in all, thought the gringo, a man did make strange companions south of the border.

His expectations for the trip took a slight turn when Tío produced two rifles. One was an old Winchester .44/.40, just like the old shoulder-buster that Hag grew up with; the other, the .30/30 that Tío had carried the day before, was of the newer model '94, which was now so popular with the sheepmen in Arizona.

"For *coyotes,*" said Tío, and the cowboy caught a double meaning in the word. For the first time he wondered if he had succeeded at entirely snuffing out the life of the sergeant.

By evening the preparations for the trip were complete. The lambs were gathered into a holding pen, Guanga was grained and watered, and the clothes and food were packed. For staples they had dried corn and goat jerky. Tío explained that goat made better jerky because it was leaner meat, and that they would eat jerky because fresh meat would spoil too quickly in the heat. Hagborn realized that killing a hundred-pound lamb on the trail, just for two men, would be extravagant. At dinner the cowboy chatted, in fragments, with Petra; anxious as he was for the morning and the trip north, he had grown rather fond of this place.

Hagborn slept lightly his second night in the stable, and he awoke to the grey of morning. He thought perhaps something had wakened him . . . he sensed another being. He slipped on his sandals. Suddenly a huge human form loomed in the light of the doorway, and in its hand there was the ominous silhouette of a pitchfork. As Hagborn came to his feet, the other man called out a question in Spanish and came towards him. The gringo lunged out of the way of the pitchfork as if he were dodging a longhorn steer. He looked around for a weapon. Near the doorway he saw a mattock, short and thick like a Southern field hoe, and he seized it as he turned to face his antagonist. The larger man now closed in slowly, feinting jabs with the fork. Hag himself feinted once with an upward swing, and as the other man brought up the pitchfork in defense, Hagborn swung the mattock back around, hooking the pitchfork head and yanking the weapon out of the man's hands. Then, to the gringo's surprise, the large Mexican turned and ran for the farmyard.

Hefting the mattock sideways, Hagborn flung it with all his might. It flew horizontally, end for end, and caught the lumbering giant behind the knees and brought him down. As the toppled man got to his knees, Hagborn tackled him. He had just worked in a chicken-wing armlock, and was pulling the man's head back by the chin, when he heard a familiar voice.

"Buenos días." Tío Boni stood there smiling.

The larger man quit struggling. Hagborn, now put at ease by the old man's merry smile, released his hold and rose to his feet. "You know this galoot?"

"*Ah, sí.* Work for me for when we go to Arizona."

"Oh." Hagborn helped the man to his feet.

"Diego," said the old man, introducing his guest to his hired man.

Hagborn shook the large man's hand, and from the dull leer on his face he realized that the man was a harmless oaf. The man gave an imbecile smile, said *"Mucho gusto,"* and returned to his morning chores.

"Who is he?" Hagborn asked of the old man.

"*Poco loco.* Pretty good man."

"What's his name?"

"Enrique Gálvez. He is called Guajolote. Turkey."

"Ah-ha," said Hagborn, and followed his host to the house.

The sun was breaking over the eastern mountains when Tío and his new trail hand stepped out of the house to begin their journey. They secured the pack, canteens, and rifles on Guanga's back, and Tío called to

Chapulín. Loosing the poles that formed the gate of the holding pen, the two men pushed the herd of sheep out of the corral. Before long, Chapulín understood the direction they would take, and he stepped out to take the lead.

The days of the great cattle drives had been over since Hag was a boy. But even though men no longer drove cattle from Texas to Wyoming and Montana, there were still shorter, regional drives made by men of Hag's calling. The methods of driving cattle had remained the same, but on a smaller scale. Now, as they bunched their little herd of sheep and pushed it in the direction of Agua Prieta, Hag remembered the vast herds of cattle he had seen when he was a boy in Texas. In their own small way — with Chapulín riding point, Hagborn riding flank, and Tío and Guanga bringing up the drag — they were making a drive. And, as with the greater herds of days past, they were heading them north!

At midday they paused in a small clump of oak trees, and the sheep settled down for a rest. As the two men sat side by side against a large trunk, Hagborn asked how the land would be.

"Halfway, pretty good. Other half, too bad. No too much water. *Tierra bronca.*"

"How about *hombres?*"

"One or two Tarahumara, *no muy malo.* No too much bad men."

"How about the Seris?" Hagborn had heard hair-raising tales of torture and cannibalism about the Seri Indians.

"No Seris. Many years past, too many Seris. Now, Seris over there." Tío waved far to the west.

"That's good," said Hagborn. "We don't need any mean Indians to bother us." In the back of his mind, however, there still nagged an uncertainty about the sergeant. And on the second evening out, the old man brought up the subject.

"Diego, you think you kill the sergeant?"

"I don't know, Tío. I never choked a man before, and the more I think about it the less I'm sure I killed him. Why do you ask?" Hagborn finished rolling his smoke and lit it.

"I think someone watch us. Maybe the sergeant, maybe other *federales.*"

"I haven't seen anybody."

"I have eyes for this country. I see just a little bit. I think Chapulín see him, too." Tío motioned with his head away from the river.

"Up in the hills?"

"Look like." The old man squinted as he

drew on his thin cigarette.

"Think we ought to be carryin' our rifles?"

"Pretty good friend." Tío's eyes twinkled as he stoked the campfire with a stick.

Throughout the next day, when Hagborn was not searching the hillsides or watching the vagabond movements of the sheep, he reflected on his own circumstances. In Arizona, herding sheep was much less respectable than working cattle. The sheepherders up there were Indians or Mexicans or Basques or Mormons; any other white sheepherders usually either had a hard luck story behind them or were too broken down to ride a horse. At the present time, though, in the company of Tío Boni, Hagborn didn't even feel down on his luck. He and Tío were helping each other out, and driving sheep was the honest work by which they were doing so. Hagborn was not, after all, riding a trail of high adventure. He only wanted to get back to the states, where he could cultivate the good habit of staying out of border towns. But his thoughts continually returned to the sergeant, and he searched the hills over and over.

And so the days wore on, Hagborn walking now this flank and now that one, with his rifle cradled in his arm. From time to time he would look back to see Tío round-ing up stragglers or yanking on Guanga's reins. On the fourth day he saw storm clouds behind them, but on the fifth day the clouds were gone.

Always in the front walked Chapulín. According to Tío, the goat knew the way as well as the old man himself, having been over the trail a dozen times before. He was as good a lead animal as any mossy-horned roan or brindle steer Hagborn had ever seen. The sheep followed him faithfully through passes and along narrow mountainside trails. He was especially useful at the river crossings, being as fearless as he was nimble.

The Río Bavispe snaked its way north through the Sierra Madre until it made a large curve to the west and then flowed south. Their route lay north, and parallel to the river. Hagborn gathered from the old man's diagram that they would leave the river at its grand curve and keep somewhat to the east where the grass was better for a while. Like many other mountain streams it was at times wide and shallow and lazy, and at other times narrow and swift. Occasionally, because of bluffs on one side or grasslands on the other, they would cross and recross the river. From time to time Tío Boni would pick out a *vado*, or crossing, that he knew of. *"Una barranca,"* he might say, pantomiming a cliff with a downward slice of the hand, or *"una vega,"* as if he were polishing a table top. In the latter case he invariably brought them to a grassy flatland where the herd could graze.

At times they would wander a few miles from the river in order to follow the better grazing. On two occasions Tío brought the herd to water at tiny reservoirs where a pool of water would be held by a rock wall. Tío called these reservoirs *trincheras,* and Hagborn could not remember having seen the likes of them anywhere but in this region of the Sierra Madre. For the most part they watered at the river, usually once a day. Always, though, one of them kept watch for the sergeant or whoever it might be that Tío suspected of trailing them.

On the sixth day of their drive, Hagborn learned that they were to leave the river and strike out across the dry and thorny mountains towards Agua Prieta. The site selected by the old man for their last crossing lay in the bottom of a canyon. Although he assured himself that Tío knew best, Hagborn sensed that this was a place rife with evil. The storm clouds they had seen to the southeast had brought the water level up and had made the current more brisk. As Hag looked around the rim, he saw shadowed crags and nooks that would easily harbor a sniper. If the old man's premonitions about the sergeant were accurate, here might be the stage for a rimrock drama.

Hag looked back to Guanga, where his sombrero and rifle were. Tío Boni was bringing up the drag, nudging the last few loitering sheep down the draw, when Hagborn urged Chapulín into the water. The goat tried his footing, plunged briefly, and took his stride swimming across. With a little more urging, Hag pushed about a dozen sheep into the water behind the billy and swam behind them. When that group was safely beached on the other side, Hagborn led Chapulín upstream, recrossed with him, and crowded together another group.

The sheep, stupid and obedient as ever, walked into the water, hit the current, and began swimming. One large lamb in the rear, however, lost its footing and its balance. As the animal went sideways, the current caught it and took it downstream backwards. The lamb thrashed, fighting for equilibrium with its head upthrust and baaing. Hagborn plunged in after it. Its tortured wail echoed and mixed with the babbling of the water as Hag lifted his own head to the surface. He reached out for the lamb and got an arm around its brisket, when suddenly the lamb's head snapped back and burst out with blood. Then Hagborn heard the crashing report of a rifle as the sound cascaded through the canyon. The ambush was on! Hag pulled the lamb around, between himself and where he judged the bullet had come from. Thus shielded, he floated downstream, jostled by rocks and snags. There came a "shloop!" in the water next to him, a jolt to the lamb's body, and the roar of two more shots.

All was silent for the space of a few seconds, then two more shots rang out. Hagborn and his dead cargo coasted around a curve, and then he hauled the body onto the north bank and scrambled for cover. He saw that the second group of sheep had crossed over safely and were now crowded together with the first group. Chapulín, curious as always, was looking across to the bank where they had come from. Suddenly Hag heard Tío Boni's voice come over the water.

"Diego!"

"Over here, Tío!"

"The bad man, he is dead!"

The old man came around the bend, picking his way along the rocks, as Hag stepped into the open by the dead lamb.

"We lost a lamb, Tío."

"One sheep, one *hombre malo*. We can eat the sheep." He grabbed a hind leg and motioned for Hag to do likewise. Together they dragged the soggy body back to the crossing.

"Where was the man with the rifle?" asked Hagborn.

"Over there," replied Tío, pointing to one of the many crevices that had boded ill to Hagborn. As the old man set himself to the task of punching the hide off the lamb, Hag climbed up the rocks to inspect the other body.

At first he did not recognize his enemy, as the army uniform had been replaced by peasant clothes. The grey shirt was stained with blood, and Hag observed where the old man had sent two slugs through the ribs. Then Hag turned the body towards him and the head lolled back, exposing two large, ugly bruises on the throat. Hagborn looked at his own two thumbs.

That evening Tío Boni broiled a leg of lamb on the northern bank of the river. "Diego," he said, poking at the coals, "in two days we pass through Agua Prieta, and into Arizona."

"It'll be nice to be free and easy again."

"Some day you come again to *México?*"

"Some day, maybe, Tío. After the revolution." Maybe someday, thought Hagborn, when the revolution was over and it was safe for a gringo to travel south of the border, he would return to Bavispe and pay a visit to Tío Boni and his laughing-eyed daughter.

IF YOU'VE GOT THE SADDLE

When I got to Lodoga I took out my rifle, dried it carefully, oiled it, and loaded it. Since morning the rain had been spotty in the foothills. In a half mile the weather could change from bright sunshine to dark grey downpour, so I had kept my rifle wrapped up. I figured the storm was pretty much passed over behind me by now, and maybe it had gotten the deer moving around. I had been eight days across the desert and through the valley, and I was getting tired of jackrabbit.

The afternoon was fresh and clean and clear after the rain. The scrub oaks and rocks stood out sharply, almost blue against the dried weeds, and the distant pines were a clear grey-green on the mountainside. I rested my rifle across my saddle, hoping the scabbard would dry out in the next couple of hours. Meanwhile I would keep an eye out for a fat buck while I thought about where I might want to make camp and get dried out.

About six or seven miles north out of Lodoga, I saw some movement down in a gully to the left of the trail. In the early autumn the deer were already turning to their grey-blue color, and for a minute I had a hard time picking out the deer in the grey trunks of the scrub oaks. Then I saw him bending his head down to nibble on acorns. He was a normal blacktail — small, with a forked horn set of antlers. I drew a bead on his neck, and I squeezed off a shot. Down he went, kicking up leaves as he tumbled into the bottom of the gully. My horse moved at that instant, too, and I had to relocate the spot where the buck had gone down. Suddenly, he was running again up on the other bank. I threw up my Winchester and put a bullet through his front shoulder. That stopped him.

I slid my rifle into the scabbard and rode down into the draw. I decided to drag the deer downhill and work on him in the bottom. I dismounted, felt for my knife to see that it was in place, and took a few quick steps to leap the channel of the gully. Just as I was clearing the trench I saw a deer lying in the bottom of the wash. I stumbled on the other side, drew myself up quick, and looked around. There was a buck in the bottom, as well as one up on the bank. Both shots had been true, and now I had twice the work ahead of me.

I didn't need even a whole deer to begin with, but I'd figured on trading off some of the meat in Glennville. It was against my principles to leave meat to go to waste, so I decided to keep both deer for trading — even if I did look like a hog. I dragged the second deer down to the bottom and went to work. I looped a rope around his hock, passed it through an oak branch up on the other bank, and tied it to the pommel of my saddle. With some gentle urging, my horse hoisted the buck up to where the front feet cleared the ground. With that method I skinned and gutted the two deer, leaving heart and liver attached inside. Both bucks had little forked horn racks, nothing to trade off for as much as a drink of whiskey, so I left the heads and hides and guts down in the muddy bottom. I tied the two deer across my saddle, wrapped in my ground sheet. Then, looking for all the world like a successful bounty hunter, I lit out on foot, leading my horse, towards Glennville.

With town still about seventeen or eighteen miles to the north, I had no intention of walking all the way that night. My gear was all damp from the storm, and I was a mite tired from wrestling those two slippery carcasses on a muddy bank. There was supposed to be a creek about six miles farther on, as I recalled. It was one of about a hundred creeks called Bear Creek, but one Bear Creek was as good as another as long as it had water and trees.

Down in a stand of cottonwoods I found a clearing that had been used as a camp before. I stripped my horse and turned him out. Finding a straight, solid branch in the deadfall I lodged it horizontally between two trees. With piggin' strings I hung up the two bucks by their hamstrings, then propped the carcasses open. Then I set camp. Before too long I had a pretty good little oak fire going. After I had laid out my gear to dry and cleaned my rifle and pistol, I leaned against a stump, rolled a cigarette, and enjoyed a tin cup of Bear Creek and Red Eye. I still felt embarrassed about my kill — over a hundred pounds of venison was quite a bit for one lone man on the trail. I would see what I could do to trade off one of the deer before I got to Glennville. Meanwhile, I trimmed out some tenderloin from along the inside of the ribs, and then I hunkered over the fire to watch it curl and broil.

By shortly after dawn the next morning, I was packed up like I had been the afternoon before. It had not been a cold night, and the sky was clear, so I expected a warm day. I hoped to cover the remaining eleven or twelve miles before the sun was straight up.

After I had walked for about two hours, I saw a likely cabin pitched up against a hillside a quarter of a mile off the road. Wood smoke was threading up out of the chimney. I gave my horse's bridle a yank, and we headed up the little trail to the cabin. Just as we ambled into what might be called the yard, a rifle barrel poked from behind a burlap flap on the left window. "Hold it right there, mister," I heard. The voice was a woman's, and it sounded a touch shaky.

"I'm friendly, ma'am," I said, as politely as I could.

"Who you got slung over that saddle?"

"Deer meat, ma'am. Thought maybe I could trade some. I ended up with more than I needed."

"You sling your gunbelt over your saddle, keep your hand off that saddle gun, and go sit over on that stump." Seeing a stump about fifteen yards to my left, I did as I was told. I rolled myself a cigarette and was licking it when the door opened.

She was of medium height and brown-haired, wearing blue cotton trousers and a red flannel shirt. They were men's clothes, but I could tell there was a shapely woman underneath. She carried an old Henry rifle.

"Hope that gun's not loaded," I said, lighting my cigarette. "If it goes off it might hurt my horse. Or me."

She didn't say anything, just walked over and lifted up an end of the ground sheet. Then she went back to the cabin, leaned the Henry against it, and turned to me.

"You got use for a whole deer?" I asked. "All I really need is a little grain for my horse, and maybe some sugar and coffee for my saddle bags."

"I'm out of fresh meat," she said, brushing the hair out of her face. "And damn tired of salt pork. Thing is, I'm low on coffee and salt and sugar myself till my . . . uh . . . man, gets back."

"I can spare the meat, even if you haven't got much to trade. I'm mostly concerned it don't go to waste, anyway." I noticed she was eyeing my cigarette. "You care for a smoke, ma'am?"

"Nope," she said. But then, apparently realizing what a poor liar she was, she said, "Sure. I haven't had one for days. I'll roll it." I tossed her my bag of makin's and finished my own cigarette as she built hers. She was pretty fair at it, even though her hands were a bit shaky. I stood up and scratched her a light, then walked over to untie my load. "Who are you?" she asked.

"No one famous," I said. "Jack Britton's the name."

"I'm Elizabeth Jensen," she said, "but I go by Betty."

I heaved one carcass over the saddle toward me. Hefting it for balance, I said, "I'll hang this for you if you show me where."

"Oh. Lean-to in back." And she scuttled off around the right side of the cabin. I followed her around back, where she was propping a rickety door open for me. I stood there waiting while she stood up on a saddle rick and ran a cord over a rafter. My arms were getting tense with the dead weight, but she was something to watch. She had the cigarette in her mouth, and the smoke was getting in her eye. Stretched out from toes to fingertips, she looked pretty fine. Finally we got the deer strung up, and she got down from her perch. She paused beside me for just a second, looked at me, and then turned and left. I went back out front to cover up the other deer and tie it back of the cantle so I could ride. She leaned out the front door and called, "Come on in when you're done there. I'll see what I can find for you."

She had a cup of coffee poured and a basin of water to wash my hands in. I never did see much future in hankerin' for another man's woman, but I got to thinking this one was all right. I was curious, to say the least. I sat down and sipped my coffee. "Where's Mr. Jensen, if I may ask?"

"There is no Mr. Jensen. There's a Mr. Burton, a Sam Burton. And he's a son of a bitch."

"Sorry. None of my business, I guess."

"That's all right. You asked an honest question. He's in Glennville, or at least that's where he said he was goin'."

"Gone long?"

"Couple of days. Not that he does much when he's here. He comes and goes."

"Look, I don't want to be pokin' into other folks' business . . ."

"I'm the one that's tellin' my life story. Forget it. All you want is some grub to trade for the venison."

"Just some grain for my horse, if you got it. I mostly didn't want to waste the deer meat, really." I sat there and sipped my coffee in silence for several minutes. She held some bitterness for this Sam Burton, and I could sense she wanted to talk about it, but I didn't want to seem eager to say anything. When my coffee was cool enough I gulped down the rest of it and pushed myself up from the table. "Bring the horse around back?" I asked.

"Yeah," she said, and went out the back

door. It was awfully uncomfortable here, but I couldn't tell if she wanted me to leave or stay. Probably a little bit of both. I think I felt the same way. I led my horse around back, where she had dumped about two pounds of oats in a feed box. My horse went to work, noisily.

"Where you going?" she asked.

I thought about saying Lodoga, but there wasn't enough reason to lie. "Glennville."

"There's a spring right over there," she said. "You can water him there." Both of us stood there, not saying anything, listening to my horse munch his oats. When he finished I led him to the spring, and she walked along. "You see," she said, "I feel like I ought to tell you. I'm sort of a kept woman." I paused at the pool, let my horse drink. I got out my tin cup and dipped a drink. It was sweet and cold. "Water's good, uh?" she asked.

"Yep," I said. "Clean and cold." I passed the cup to her and she took a sip.

"I'm not exactly his wife," she said, returning to her earlier line, "but he's treated me like one. You know, I was half hoping that was him you had tied down on your saddle. If I had a way out of here I'd take it."

"Does he keep you here against your

will?" I felt like I'd just asked a real stupid question.

"I just don't have any way to leave. No horse. If I left on foot he'd catch me and beat me."

"Hmmm . . . ," I said, "I don't imagine you want to ride to Glennville with me." I really didn't want to walk the rest of the way, anyway.

"No," she said, "I don't think so." She took another sip and handed me the cup. "Where you going after Glennville?"

"Haven't decided," I said. "I got a debt to pay there, and after that I'm either going up to Oregon or back to Colorado."

"Mister," she said, "if you come back through here, and you help me out of here, I'll make it right to you some day." She looked me square in the eye, and her face twitched like she was going to cry. "Decently," she said.

"You put me in a spot," I answered. "I don't know this Sam Burton, or you either, for that matter. But I like you." At that moment she turned slightly towards me, and I moved towards her. Her lips were cold from the tin cup, but beneath the cold there was warmth. My right hand still held the cup as I gently crushed her upper body against mine. My left hand rested on her snug waist. As we separated, I moved my right hand to rest on the other side of her waist. "If I'm not back in two days," I said, "I'd like to be remembered as a gentleman." I kissed her lightly and then pulled myself away before I got into any more trouble. I shook out the cup, tossed it in my saddlebag, and led my horse back out onto the trail. I stepped into the stirrup, swung my leg over the deer, and nudged my horse into a fast walk.

Glennville lay warming under a midday Indian summer sun. It seemed like I'd gotten there in no time, I'd had so much to think about. There was my "debt" to pay, there was the possibility of running into Sam Burton, and there was that nagging tug at me to ride back down the same trail when I finished here.

I had come from Colorado to make Jeff Haskins either take water or take a beating. He had left me in the mountains east of Grand Junction. I awoke the morning after I was shot, and he was gone. He had taken my rifle, my cartridges, and my canteen. When I got to Grand Junction, with the grace of God and the help of an outcast Mormon, I swore I would trail him and find him. And punish him at last. Time and good health had healed the gunshot wound, but three years hadn't cooled my anger. A drink of cold spring water, though, and the cold, warm lips of a woman had changed my view a little. For reasons I couldn't put a finger on, no matter how much I searched, I believed in her. It wasn't just the warm and probably willing body of a woman, although that no doubt had some effect. Nor was it the urge to make an honest woman of her, to raise her up from the street to start a new life. I'd seen too many self-important men make fools of themselves with that attitude. No, there was something behind that look on her face — a deep, cool decency. I would have bet a gold eagle right then that her rifle had been loaded.

Regardless of whether I went north or south I would need supplies, so I went about the business of chiselling and bartering with the storekeeper. I kept back a couple of loin steaks, and after packing away my new provisions in my saddlebags I took the steaks to the cook of the Buckeye Saloon. I asked him to cook up an order of potatoes and onions to go along, and I strolled out to the bar. To whet my appetite I sipped on your standard three fingers of Red Eye and minded my own business. I wanted to know about Sam Burton, and about Jeff Haskins, but I wanted to eat first and take care of business as casually as possible.

It's hard to ruin a good steak, but the cook in the Buckeye did his damnedest. I scraped off some of the burned crust and went at my meal. Despite their looks, the potatoes and onions were pretty good eating. When the bartender came over to pour me another drink, he asked the usual question.

"Passin' through?"

"Goin' to Oregon."

"What brings you through this way?"

"Oh, it wasn't too much out of the way, and I heard an old trail pard of mine had settled here."

"What's he go by?"

"Jeff Haskins when I knew him."

"Oh, yeah. Got one arm."

"Don't know about that."

"Yeah, he comes into town once in a while. He lives up on the Sugarloaf. Him and his woman. Used to be a miner's woman, and I think the miner got the best of that deal."

"What's he do for a living?"

"Oh, he grubs out a livin' by doin' a little trappin', a little huntin'. Seems like every once in a while he finds a horse to sell." That sounded about like what you could expect from Jeff. "You say you're a friend of his?" The barkeep seemed like maybe he felt he'd stepped out of line by running down one of my friends.

"Not exactly," I said, putting him at ease. "Just someone I used to know."

"Umph. Well, if you got a mind to look him up, you'll likely find him out there on the Sugarloaf."

"Thanks." It didn't exactly please me to hear what a lousy life Jeff had ended up in, but I was getting that relieved feeling that maybe he didn't need me to punish him. I didn't want to gloat over another man's misfortune, but I did feel satisfied. Maybe I'd leave it at that.

The Glennville Hotel had the other bar in town, so I thought I'd go there for the second half of my gossip. Jeff Haskins wasn't nagging at my mind nearly so much as that woman was, and I was interested in knowing more about Sam Burton. I was hoping to find out about him without mentioning his name, but I wasn't sure how to go about it.

As I stepped out onto the board sidewalk, a little commotion down the street caught my attention. Getting closer I saw that two men were arguing, and as I joined the small crowd of onlookers I recognized one of the two men as Jeff Haskins. His general appearance — hair, beard, clothes, and stubbed arm — assured me he'd gone downhill since I'd seen him. He was arguing with a large, burly man about a horse.

"You owe me forty dollars, and I want my money." Haskins' voice was somewhere between a snarl and a whine.

"The hell I do. You owe me a horse from the last string I bought from you. I had to shoot that worthless claybank. I'll take this paloose, and you'll like it." The larger man was pointing a rifle, with one hand, to emphasize his argument.

"Why, you'd cheat your own mother out of —"

The larger man backhanded Haskins with the barrel of his rifle, and the beaded sight cut a gash on his face as the blow knocked him to the ground. The big man kicked him in the ribs, and Haskins squirmed. Writhing, Haskins caused the second kick to miss its aim and hit him on the stump of his arm. He screamed in pain and looked around to beg for help. When our eyes met he quit screaming; he just crawled towards his horse. I turned and walked to the Glennville Hotel.

As I took my place at the bar, several of the other onlookers filed back in to their places at the bar and the card table. I clinked a five-dollar gold piece on the bar.

The bartender looked like he might have been a card player or maybe still was. He was clean-shaven and neatly dressed, with smooth hands. He didn't make a flourish to pour a drink like some bartenders do — his hands glided from bottle to glass to till to bar rag. I don't recall ever meeting a man who could be so shrewd without leaning on you. When I was half way through my drink he paused in front of me, polishing a glass. Ever so quietly, and with a helpful tone to his voice, he asked, "Who you lookin' for?"

I almost knocked my drink over. I looked at him. Right then I could tell he didn't much care about anybody's personal life, but he was very interested in whatever went on in his bar. He also struck me as a man who kept most things under his hat, unlike the man across the street. "Sam Burton," I said softly.

"That's better than havin' him lookin' for you." He smiled, walked down to the other end of the bar, and came back to light a tailor-made cigarette. "You can tell he's not looking for anyone. That's him in the grey shirt, playing stud." He shook out the match and nodded slightly towards the card game. "Good card player, too," he added. I slowly turned to see the man who had just kicked around Jeff Haskins. He was playing cards and looking calm. This would take some thought.

I finished my drink slowly and ordered another. "Get yourself one, too," I said, leaving a dollar on the counter as I stood up. I headed towards the game.

"Thanks," he said, in that same silk-smooth voice.

Just as I was nearing the card table I heard Burton speak. "Degnan," he said, "I'd rather have a sister that worked in a whore-house than a brother that dealt cards like you do." A merry little chuckle went around the card table as I looked at the dealer. He was a red-faced little chap with shaky hands, who looked like he let nothing bother him. Nothing except maybe the need for a drink.

"Seat open, mister," said Degnan.

"Friendly game," chimed in one of the players.

The empty seat was two places to Burton's right, and that suited me. I wouldn't really meet him head on unless I did a lot of raising. I wasn't that deadly a hand at maverick stud anyway, which was what they were playing. I bought ten dollars' worth of chips and sat down.

My second impression of Sam Burton was that he was neither a dirty man nor a clean one. He was one of those men who would always look like they had bathed and shaved two days ago. I also knew, from the general state of his cabin, that he was not a man proud of the things he built or made. Now, from observing the neat stacks of blue, red, and black chips, I could tell he was proud of the things he owned. As the game progressed I watched his betting, like anyone can be expected to do. "Not worth five dollars," he would say, or "I'm not that proud of a couple of whores," when he threw in his hand. And once, shortly after he had tossed in the pair of queens, he had two kings showing. "You know, Beaver," he said to his opponent, "I think my cowboys can ride roughshod over your two pair." He raised five dollars, waited for Beaver to fold, and reached out with both hands to drag in the chips. A man who closely gauged the value of anything you had, in comparison with anything he had, most likely fixed a firm price on horses, guns, and women. Probably in that order.

He didn't win every hand he played — no card player does. But unlike the sharpest card players, like maybe the bartender, he didn't lay back and let another player drag a pot. When he had finally busted Beaver out of the game, an accomplishment he seemed mildly proud of, he summed himself up to me. He tossed twenty dollars' worth of chips across the table, as if to buy the man himself. "Here's a personal loan, Beaver. You can pay me when you sell your skins." Then he turned to the man sitting between us and said, "I don't need the money all that bad. I just like to win."

After he loaned out the twenty dollars, though, his winning streak seemed to end. He looked at my stack, which had absorbed some of his and most of Beaver's second stake. In about two hours I had run my stack up to almost fifty dollars.

"Say, stranger," he said to me, "what would it take to get that money back in the game? You seem to be sittin' on that stack."

"I think my streak went cold," I answered, "and I don't feel like throwing it away."

"No one's asking you to be a fool."

"Do I understand, then, that you have a horse for sale?"

"Bareback appaloosa, tied up out front. Go take a look."

It was still light outside, and the horse looked fine to me. Neither of them had had it long enough to ruin it. I walked back in and stacked my chips in tens. "Didn't I hear it described as a forty-dollar horse?"

"You did." He didn't seem ruffled about the Haskins incident.

"Well, here's forty," I said, setting the four stacks in front of him.

"Horse's yours," he said. He didn't even offer to shake on it.

In the next few hands I dwindled away the other seven dollars. When I got up and left, he ignored me.

The sun was going down in a clear sky when I walked out into the street. I remembered how she had looked at me when she had said the word "decently," and I imagined how little the notion of decency had touched his life. As for myself, I felt like doing something clean. I felt as if my grudge against Jeff Haskins had been washed away, or at least taken care of, and I felt no particular hatred for Sam Burton. I just felt as if I had brushed up against something soiled, and I wanted to get out in the clean air.

Two hours later I trotted into the yard of her cabin, leading the horse. A patch of light shot out as a corner of the burlap lifted.

"Who is it?" she called out.

"Who do you think?" I called back.

The door opened as I was stepping out of the stirrup. I took her in my arms and pressed her against me. "You're back," she murmured into my shirt. I put my hands on her shoulders and held her back in the light.

"Have you got a saddle?" I asked. "I've got the horse."

Before the moon was high we had packed her things and had taken down the remaining venison. "Thank the good Lord," I thought as I was tying it down, "for the second buck down in that draw."

That night, in the clear moonlight, we rode stirrup to stirrup back through Lodoga and down through the rain-washed hills.

STONE IN THE DISTANCE

The cold, clear stillness of morning filled the void as he awoke in his bed on the ground. Things of the world came to him — the shift of his horse's hooves, the drag of the picket rope across the grass, the rough texture of the saddle blanket that separated him from the hard ground. He opened his eyes on the new day, which was grey still in the shadow of the mountain. Today would be another day like the last few, measured by the amount of country he would cover. He thought of himself as a form, together with his horse, moving across the face of the earth a day at a time.

Covered by a wool blanket and his oilskin slicker, he had slept in his clothes. Rolling out into the morning, then, was a matter of putting on his hat and boots. He took the horse to water at the little stream nearby, where he washed his hands and face upstream from the horse's gentle slurping.

With the can left over from the peaches that had been his supper, he dipped water for coffee. He made a fire with the small cedar branches he had gathered the night before, and as the fire crackled he leaned towards it and took in the warmth. It was early spring. He thought of the trees leafing out and the fruit trees blooming along the valley of the Rio Grande. That was behind him. Here on Ratón Pass it was chilly, and as he traveled northward he would be moving on the verge of spring. Fair weather came later on the northern high plains, and later still in the mountains of Wyoming, Idaho, and Montana. Time wasn't standing still, but the slow change of climate would go along with his slow passage.

After a breakfast of coffee and cold hard biscuits, he flattened the can and tossed it into the coals. With the instep of his boot he dragged the damp red dirt back into the little pit he had scraped out. Then he found a rock, a field stone about a foot across and four inches thick, and dropped it flat on top of where his fire had been.

The sun was rising and the shadows were moving as he saddled the horse, tied on his bedroll and saddlebags, took a look around the campsite, and led the horse back out onto the trail. He knew that somewhere along this part of the pass, there was an imaginary line separating New Mexico Territory and the state of Colorado. Maybe he had crossed the line the evening before, and maybe he would cross it sometime this morning. Either way, the valley of the Rio Grande was at his back; and the person he had been, Andrew Newton, was back there too, dead before his time, without so much as a headstone.

Since the day he had decided to make his break, which had been less than a week earlier, he had kept himself looking straight ahead. To get sentimental, or to backtrack, could be fatal. He decided he would have to follow through, keeping a cool head and not dilly-dallying. If he was ever going to break from the gang and get out alive, now was the time, with the Sanger brothers in jail. When they got out, which would be sooner or later, they would look for him. He hoped that by then the winds and rains of time would have brushed out his tracks.

He thought he had done things in a pretty good order, starting with things that could talk. It had been hard to say good-bye to Sarah. He could still see her, her blue eyes shining in fear, her blonde hair sticking to her tear-dampened cheeks. She had wanted to go, and then she had promised to wait for him. In response to both pleas he had been firm. "No," he said, "it can't be. For your good, and for your family's. If all you know is that I'm gone, it'll be easier." He told her about the McGuire kid, and how the Sangers had tormented the family until they finally found where the kid was hiding.

After Sarah it had been his horse and saddle — first the saddle, with his initials stamped in the leather. He sold it in one saddle shop in Santa Fe and then went to another to buy the old, worn, nondescript saddle he now used. Then it was the horse, the same way. He had liked having a handsome horse and outfit, but the chestnut with four white socks and blaze was nearly as loud as the initials on the saddle. He sold the horse a little cheap, went across town, and bought a thick-built, dull-brown horse. It had a brand on the front right shoulder, a diamond with a cross in it, which wasn't a known brand thereabouts. The stable man said it was a northern brand. He guaranteed it was all clean and said he could write a bill of sale. Andy nodded and gave his name as T.J. Stubblefield.

The brown horse was a good walker. He had probably seen a lot of country and probably didn't mind going back north, if that was where he was from.

It had been tough to trade in the good-looking horse and outfit for the drab and dull. It had also been hard to say good-bye to Sarah, to give up something that neither of them wanted to end. Harder still, as he tried to put it all behind him, was the idea of giving up his own name. He liked his name and had never been ashamed of it, but now he had to slip out of a tight spot. It was of his own making, getting mixed up with the Sanger brothers. He had heard it called riding the lariat trail — the trail that started with a wide loop and maybe ended with a narrow one. If he was going to clean up and go straight, that meant getting rid of anything that tied him to his early life and name. So he was T.J. Stubblefield in passage, for as long as he rode the horse with the diamond-cross brand.

He knew he could have gone east and north to one of the big cities like Chicago or New York, where he could have lost himself in the crowd. But he had left home in Iowa and had gone west at sixteen, and after eight years in the great wide open, he knew it was the only life for him. He knew there was ranch work in the timbered ranges of the north. He imagined the region as a billowy, dark-green ocean. If he could drop into the middle of it, he might feel free enough to start life over and do it right.

He followed the trail north for over a week

more, keeping to himself but not hiding or doing anything that he thought would be memorable. One night he found a rock overhang to sleep under, but the rest of the nights he slept in the open. The trail followed the western edge of the plains, with the front range of the Rockies always on his left. It was big country, and each day he put a little more of it behind him.

Sometimes he felt sharply the pang of having left everything. Maybe in the process of making camp he wished he still had a hatchet, or in the morning he would remember what it had been like to be able to choose between a coat and a jacket. Such a little detail would trigger a sense of the total loss and dispossession, the denial of everything he had had and had been. All of those things that he used to have in one place — not many, but enough to have loaded a packhorse — all of those things were scattered around now. He who had been the center of that life was now traveling light on a good-walking horse.

North of Denver, he had his first noteworthy encounter with another traveler. It was during his mid-day rest when he saw the other man turn off the trail to stop and visit.

Stubblefield, he told himself, as he had

been in the habit of doing. *I'm T.J. Stubblefield.*

The brown horse was stripped and picketed, facing north and grazing. Its back showed the matted, fringed outline of the saddle and blanket. The horse had been shedding in the spring weather, and the brand stood out clearly.

"Good afternoon," said the man as he rode up on a black horse.

"Good afternoon."

"Name's Wilson," the man said as he touched his hat brim. He had grey eyes and a clean-shaven face, and he looked to be about thirty-five.

"Stubblefield's mine. Pleased to meet you."

"Likewise." The man made no move toward getting off his horse. "Spring's comin' on," he said.

"Yes, it is."

The man in the saddle smiled, in no apparent hurry. He looked across at the brown horse and said, "Diamond-cross."

A nod.

"You didn't ride for them, did you?"

"No, I bought that horse." He had already decided not to let himself get crossed up. He would have liked to say he bought the horse in Denver, but the bill of sale said

Santa Fe. If pressed, he would eventually have to let it be known he came from there. So, to avoid volunteering any details, he motioned with his head and said, " 'Way south."

The stranger had both hands on the saddle horn. "You'll see those horses all over now." He turned down the corners of his mouth and nodded.

"Is that right?"

"Yep. It was a good-sized outfit, up in the Niobrara country." The man nodded as he spoke.

"Where's that?"

"Way north of here and a little east, what they call the sandhills, where that outfit was. They sold out, a couple of years ago."

"Uh-huh."

"But not too long before that, someone made off with a herd of them diamond-cross horses." The man pointed his chin towards the brown horse.

"Is that right? I'm glad I've got a bill of sale on this one."

"Always a good idea. I don't think anyone's makin' any trouble over them horses now, anyway, but it's a good thing to know about." The man smiled.

"Well, I sure appreciate it. There's

enough trouble in this world without a man goin' lookin' for it."

The man smiled again. "Isn't that the truth." Then he tugged his hat and said, "Well, I'd better get movin'." He seemed about to touch spurs to the black horse when he paused and said, "You'll find a good stream north of here in time to camp tonight, if you're goin' north."

"I am."

"It's a good spot. I camped there last night. Then it's a good day's ride from there on into Cheyenne." He glanced at the horse, then touched his hat and said, "Nice meetin' you."

"And the same here."

T.J. Stubblefield watched as the man called Wilson rode away on the dark horse. He wondered if the man was some sort of range detective, the way he ferreted out information. Might be, with a soft touch and friendly way. Or he just might be the kind of fellow who talked to everyone on the trail. That could be worse.

Stubblefield, Sommerfield, what the hell's the difference, he thought as he saddled up. *I've got to get rid of this horse. And I'll be damned if I'll camp where he said.*

He pushed the brown horse north, coming to the creek in late afternoon. There was good grass there, so he let the horse graze for an hour. Resting against the saddle where he had set it on the ground, he turned and looked back down the trail.

Damn the luck, he thought. *The best thing in the world would be to take this horse back to Denver and trade it off.* But two things kept him from doing it. He might bump into Wilson, after having told him he was going north. Furthermore, it would be back-tracking, and he had made up his mind he wasn't going to do any of that.

He looked at the horse. It was a good horse, and he had even thought of keeping it for a while. The other idea he'd had was to trade it off in Cheyenne or a little farther along the way. But if everybody knew these horses and everybody noticed them, he would put himself on the map by either keeping it or trading it. He saddled the horse for the third time that day and pushed on, riding another ten miles before making a dry camp at nightfall.

Damn it, he thought, as he sat by his campfire. Someone — a man who liked to talk — had the name of Stubblefield and the diamond-cross horse connected with his description. He looked at the horse, grazing at the edge of the firelight. It wasn't the horse's fault, but it was a problem. Maybe it was just a mental problem, he reasoned with himself — maybe he just thought the eyes of the world were on him. Then he shook his head. Peace of mind was what was at stake here, not whether he had done anything wrong or whether anyone was even likely to follow him this far. For the purpose of trying to achieve peace of mind he had erased Andrew Newton. Now he was going to have to erase Stubblefield and the diamond-cross horse. They came together, and they would go together.

It was late afternoon the next day when he drew rein on the hill overlooking Cheyenne. He had been riding due north for a little over two weeks. The railroad ran west from here, all the way to the coast. It could take him to Salt Lake City, and from there he could go north again to Idaho or Montana. He looked off to the west. If he could get on the train here without a great deal of attention, he could jump five hundred miles and leave not a trace.

He patted the brown horse on the neck. It was a good horse and had taken him a long way, but he had to let go of it. For as long as he rode it, he was Stubblefield upon question. If he sold it, he lodged himself and that name into someone else's memory. If he turned it free, it would be a loose detail that would eat at him and leave him no rest. At this point it was not a matter of whether the horse would tell tales on him, but a matter of what circumstances he could live with.

What he had in mind could be done anywhere out of town, so he skirted Cheyenne and rode towards the north. Picking an area midway between the railroad that angled northwest and the trail that ran northeast, he came to a brushy draw, where he stopped. Seeing no one in any direction, he dismounted and pulled the saddle from the horse. He stashed the gear in the brush and then hoisted himself onto the horse bareback.

Nerve-strung but determined, he rode the horse for another mile. When he found a narrow draw that looked right, he stopped and slid off. Holding the reins with his left hand, he stood facing the horse. He tugged it one way and the other until he had it standing uphill in the cleft of the draw. Then he drew his six-shooter, cocked it as he placed the muzzle beneath and between the lower jawbones, and pulled the trigger.

The world seemed to come apart, with the roar of the pistol and the backward explosion of the horse, which reared screaming and pawing. The man was pulled forward, then the bridle gave, and he found himself sitting with legs spraddled and the bridle in his lap, as the ground jarred with the impact of the falling horse. The animal was snorting and groaning into the dust, just four feet away, with its legs thrashing. A second pistol shot stilled the horse.

It had fallen right side up, brand showing. For that reason he had chosen the site he had. On the sloping ground, it would be possible to flop the horse over.

He had not cried when he had left Sarah, nor on Ratón Pass when he had left his name and his whole life behind him. But he felt tears in his eyes and a choke in his throat as he said, "I'm sorry," to the horse with no name and a diamond-cross brand.

Turning the carcass over wore him out, partly because of the dead, sloppy weight of the horse, and partly because of the toll that the ordeal took on his nerves. Finally, after a long battle of tugging and lifting, he got the job done.

By the time he made his way back to his saddle and gear, he felt wrung out. He rested a little while, fiddling with his gear until the sun went down. The headstall had been cut by the bullet, so that part of the bridle was no good. That was why it had come off in his hand. He salvaged the bit and reins, tucking them into the saddlebags. After tying the saddle blanket on with the bedroll, snugging the cinches, and tying the stirrups together across the seat, he figured it was time to go. He lifted the saddle by the underside of the swells and slung it onto the back of his right shoulder. Then he started walking towards Cheyenne.

At one point he thought he should have cut out the part of the hide that had the brand, but he reasoned that no one would be so interested as to turn over a dead horse — and if someone did, it would be better not to have left any cause for suspicion.

He rented a cheap, stuffy room in a hotel near the train station. Cowboys came and went with their saddles in this town, so he felt quite normal-looking as he checked in. He signed the register "B.W. Goings."

Once in the room, he opened a window for fresh air. He heard the sounds of the dance halls and saloons, and the thought of the dance hall girls, which ordinarily would have struck a spark, did nothing. There was still a thickness in his throat as he thought of the brown horse, which would now be turning cold and stiff out on the prairie north of town.

It was his fault, he told himself, for even being in this spot. Once he had come this far, it was the only way he could get out and feel as if he had some control. Still, for all that it seemed necessary, it wasn't right.

He could not remember ever having prayed before, but he knelt at the edge of the bed in the cheap hotel room, and facing north, he repented again to the horse. "I'm sorry. It wasn't your fault. I had to be hard. I hope it's the last thing like that I ever do."

In the morning when he got up and moved around, his mind was fixed on the west. Now he wanted even more strongly to make the big jump. He wanted to be like a stone tossed out into a pond. Yes, that was it — a common stone.

In Salt Lake he would buy a horse to ride north. He would treat it well. He had always treated horses well, even this one, until it came time to burn bridges. Now he was determined more than ever to start over new and clean; he owed it to the horse. Otherwise, the horse would have died for nothing.

After checking out at the desk, he shouldered the saddle that belonged to no one in particular. He walked to the train station and set down the burden as he ordered and paid for a ticket to Salt Lake City. The ticket agent said the train would arrive in two hours.

"Could I leave my saddle here while I go get a bite to eat?"

"Sure. I can put it behind the counter." The agent tore a scrap of paper from a larger sheet. "I'll put your name on it." The ticket man poised his pencil over the scrap of paper and glanced up. "Name?"

He thought quickly. This one could be for keeps. Then he said, "Stone. Jim Stone."

FLOWERS FOR REBECCA

Toward the end of March, along about sundown of a day that had nearly reached seventy degrees, Ned Porter made a discovery. He was looking at the two young ash trees on the parcel where he had lived all winter, and he found that one was alive and limber while the other was dry and stiff. Any ash trees were a long way yet from leafing out, but he could tell that one was alive and one was dead. He looked up and down the dead one, about ten feet tall like its partner, and he saw twigs for kindling along with an armful of stove wood. He looked at the other and saw the prospect of shade. That was why old McIver had planted them on the west side, Ned supposed — for shade. Then he made his discovery. Bending a dry branch and then a live one, to compare the resiliency, he discovered that the live tree was colder to the touch. The dead one was warm, as the day had been, while the live one was cold, as the nights had been. He hadn't paid that much attention to plant life before.

Two nights later it snowed, a wet and

heavy spring snow. Then the weather warmed up again, and as it did, Ned saw the first green shoots in the flower beds. All winter long, he had shook out his coffee grounds by the front door, which faced south. He had been vaguely aware that there were flower beds up against the house, just as he had had a general notion that McIver had been a queer old bird. What Ned hadn't realized was that the flowers would come back; and here they were, pale green tips pushing up through the shrinking cover of snow. Well, that was fine, he thought, but he'd be damned if he was going to do anything for them. He knew of people, the likes that lived in town, that would be watering and weeding and such.

Old Vernon McIver must have been that way. But he was dead and gone, and the way Ned felt, if a plant or animal didn't have a use, it was on its own. Plants were for grub, graze, shade, and firewood; animals were for hides or meat or work. That was the way it was, as Ned saw things. It was said that old McIver had kept a pet burro at one time and, even though he always kept a shotgun loaded, he never killed a cottontail — that, and he brought wild rose bushes up from the gullies and then pumped water to haul to them. He was a queer old bird, all right.

Ned smiled. He'd eaten half a dozen cottontails that winter, sometimes shooting them from the doorway. And on one winter morning he had dropped a big Canada goose from a flock overhead. The heavy bird spiraled down and thumped right by the hitching rail. Take it that way when you can get it, he thought, because the hard times will make up for it. People could grow flowers and keep pets and hunt for sport if they wanted — and play the violin too, for all he cared.

On Saturday nights, Ned rode his horse, Baldy, to town, where he could have a few drinks, play cards, and sometimes be with a woman. Other times he did nothing more than nurse a slow drink and chat with young fellows like himself. Several of them had grown up right here in Grover and knew all the stories. That's how he came to hear about the burro, the wild roses, the tulips, and a woman called Rebecca.

As the story went, McIver had been crazy in love with this woman Rebecca. When he first came to town, over twenty years earlier, he talked about Rebecca. She lived down in Utah, and she was going to come to join him as soon as he got things settled. She had dark hair and blue eyes, he said, and she played the piano. She was pretty, and they were going to have a family.

McIver got a job in the train yard, bought the parcel out on the other side of Buffalo Head Creek, and built the little house. He built it facing south-southwest, towards Utah, and he planted flowers. The next year he planted more flowers, and lilac bushes, and apple trees that died. After a couple of years, people noticed he didn't talk about her any more. And no dark-haired, blue-eyed woman named Rebecca ever came to Grover.

It was said that McIver went thin and turned grey all in a year, while he was still in his thirties, and then looked about the same for the next twenty years. Then he died. He lay down to take a little nap one afternoon after dinner, in the shade of a boxcar, and he never woke up.

That was the story of McIver, plus a few other details here and there, as Ned pieced it all together. Now, as the green shoots were pushing up through the melting snow, Ned began to take an interest in the story. He wondered why Rebecca never came, and he wondered whether McIver was a little addled in the head.

The green shoots, which he understood came from bulbs down below, were of two kinds. The darker ones were long and slender, not as bright as onion tops, and not as tubular. They bloomed first, in early April — bright, yellow, rich-smelling, trumpet-shaped blossoms. Ned learned that they were daffodils. The paler shoots were broad, triangular, coming to a pointed tip. They bloomed scarlet, red, and yellow. Ned recognized them as tulips and found them nearly odorless.

It was surprising to see such life and color, after a long winter of grey and tan and white. Ned realized that the life beneath the flowers had been there with him through the winter, all the times he had pitched his coffee grounds, shot rabbits, or stepped outside to relieve himself. He also realized that the meadowlarks, whose tinkling song he heard when he saddled his horse each morning, had come with the springtime.

When the lilacs bloomed in the middle of May, Ned had a strong sense of being connected with the earlier life of the place. He knew McIver was dead, and he didn't believe in ghosts, but he felt the presence of the older man. The perfume of the lilacs conveyed the feeling that old McIver had seen the same soft purple clusters and had savored the same rich smell that he, Ned, was now taking in. He imagined the sad man still linked to this place, to this house he had built, to these flowers he had cultivated for Rebecca.

Ned smiled as he plucked a grouse he had shot for supper. He thought, that lilac perfume is making me crazy. The whole world is coming on green, the air seems alive, and I'm sticking my nose in the lilac blossoms. No wonder McIver ended up the way he did.

Still, Ned knew that he had to find out more about the woman named Rebecca.

His friends told him about an old woman, a widow with the last name of Hogan, who had known McIver as well as anyone might have. Ned found out where she lived in town, and he went to see her.

She was not as old as he had expected, but she was probably in her middle sixties. She had long grey hair plaited in a braid that lay down the middle of her back, a grey braid against black knitted wool as Ned followed her into her parlor. She sat opposite him in a matching cane-back chair.

"Yes," she said, "Vernon McIver lived a sad and lonely life. But he was a good man, and those of us still alive who knew him, we miss him."

"I never met him, but living on his place, I've gotten to feelin' as if I know him."

Mrs. Hogan's eyebrows widened upwards, as if she expected information.

"Nothing personal, really. I mean, I didn't find anything he left behind, but now with the flowers blooming —"

Her face relaxed into a smile. "Oh, yes," she said, "he was fond of his flowers. Proud of them."

"They tell me he planted them for a woman. Someone named Rebecca."

The smile receded. She nodded but left it to him to say more.

He licked his dry lips. "And I guess it's made me curious. Made me wonder."

"Well," Mrs. Hogan said, "you've probably heard as much of the story as anyone has, but I can try to answer any questions that might be bothering you." Then she said no more, as if waiting.

Ned thought for a minute. Then he said, "I guess I wonder why he cared so much for her, and why she never came."

"Vernon loved her," she said.

"Well, yes."

"He loved her, and he knew she loved him," she said, in the tone that a person might take to defend a relative. "But another man came between them."

"I didn't hear that."

"It wasn't pleasant for him, but it wasn't

anything he tried to hide, at least not the way he told the story to his friends."

Ned pondered it for a moment. "This other man, did he come between them while Vernon was here waiting for her?"

"No, before. Vernon was working on the railroad, and the other man told her he was dead. Then the man talked her into marrying him, and he moved her off to Utah."

"Where were they before?"

"Down in New Mexico."

"Vernon too?"

"Yes, both of them."

"And so he came here?"

"Yes, he knew railroading, so he came here."

"And he expected her to run away from her husband?"

"It wasn't quite the way it sounds. She was going to try to get her marriage annulled."

"And he waited."

"Yes, he waited and hoped and worried himself sick."

"For twenty years?"

"No, for about two years. Then she wrote him and told him not to wait any more."

"Did she just give up?"

"In a way, I suppose. She had a baby, and Utah would have been a hard place to get out of a marriage, anyway."

"Did he give up?"

Mrs. Hogan seemed to be speaking more comfortably now. "I wouldn't say so. It had already taken its toll on him, and the solitary life had pretty well grown on him — sort of become a habit with him."

Ned paused. "Do you think he was still waiting for all those years?"

"In a way, I suppose. It was probably part habit and part hope."

"That's a sad story."

"Yes, it is. And he never spoke ill of her."

"Why should he?"

Mrs. Hogan seemed to grow cold for just an instant as she said, "Well, she did ask him to wait for the first two years or so, and promised him in letter after letter —"

Ned must have looked startled, for she seemed to back up before going on.

"No, I didn't read any letters, but when he would get one he would come by and tell me how his hopes had been re-kindled. My husband was alive then, and we were the friends Vernon confided in. Then after he got the last letter he didn't talk much about her any more. I think he kept all the letters for a few more years at least, but I know they weren't around when he died."

"Oh?"

"No. He told me, a couple of years earlier, that he had gotten rid of everything."

"Except the flowers."

Mrs. Hogan's eyes watered. "He loved his flowers."

After the lilacs, on into the month of June, Ned watched the wild roses. They bloomed for nearly three weeks, their dainty pink blossoms smiling as the sun grew warmer. Some of the flowers curled to form a cup, while on others the petals lay flat and fragile-looking. In a heavy afternoon rain or a strong wind, the pink petals littered the ground.

His greatest surprise came while the wild roses were still in bloom, in early June. A few yards from the house, off in the direction of the gully where Vernon McIver had thrown his rubbish, Ned found a pincushion cactus by the footpath. It was a double cactus, but smaller than a woman's fist, and it had a double magenta-colored blossom growing out of its heart.

He heard himself saying Mrs. Hogan's words. "He loved her."

For a short while after that, the pink roses and blue flax bloomed together. The flowers were about the same size and grew to about the same height, and as Ned looked from a clump of flax to a stand of roses, it was as if he was looking at little beings. Then the roses were done, and the flax bloomed on. As Ned would learn, the flax would last for several weeks. Every morning, a new bouquet of firm, five-petaled flowers would appear, and when the day turned warm and dry, the blue petals would shower the ground, to be replaced with fresh ones the next morning.

That was the way it must have been with Vernon, he thought — hope reborn every day, love renewed with every spring, a man made helpless every time the lilacs bloomed. That was the way it seemed, this message as he read it from old McIver's hand.

One day in August, when the blue flax blossoms seemed to be thinning out, Ned decided to visit Mrs. Hogan again. This time they sat on her shady porch.

"I suppose you're still curious about Vernon," she said.

"And about her, too. I wonder if she's still alive."

"She very well could be."

"I wonder if she knows, or ever knew."

"Knew what?"

"How much he cared."

Mrs. Hogan nodded, her face showing agreement. "Oh, yes," she said.

"Or that he's gone now."

She shrugged.

"I wish I knew how to find her," he said. "I wish I knew her full name, and where she lived."

Mrs. Hogan shook her head.

Ned looked at her. "No?"

She shook her head again. "It wouldn't do any good even if you could find her. And for all we know, her name might not even have been Rebecca. She was a married woman, you remember."

No rain fell that August. The tulip stalks were collapsed and turning brown, and the daffodil shoots were falling over. The red rose hips hung like tiny tomatoes where the pink blossoms had smiled. The flax plants still stood brisk and green, but even they had gone to seed, the center strands bowed with their little berry-like husks. Ned looked at the parched ground, dry and crusty in the summer heat. A velvet ant, the kind he had learned to call cow ants back home, crawled through the curly dry buffalo grass. Ned looked at the wilting flower beds, the drooping leaves on the wild rose canes, the flowerless flax, and the dry, dusty leaves of the lilac bushes. It was a tired scene, but not without hope. He knew that beneath the ground there was the force of life, and as he looked at the blossomless plants he could imagine next year's flowers.

Ned smiled to himself as he set old McIver's tin bucket beneath the hand pump in the kitchen, poured a cup of water down the prime hole, and started working the handle.

SPRING COMES TO THE WIDOW

Sam Fontaine was riding south when he found the death camp. The breeze was blowing north from a small stand of junipers, and he caught his first whiff nearly a quarter of a mile away.

He had ridden north all spring and summer, eating dust and fighting flies, to deliver a trail herd in Montana. When the boss paid them off, Sam bought his favorite horse out of the remuda before the string was sold. Rather than go on a spree with the boys, Sam turned the good horse Sandy straight back south and rode alone, a season's wages in his pocket, a lightness in his heart, and a song on his lips.

The lightness and the song ended when he smelled death. It was never a good smell, but if a fellow saw what it was before he smelled it, things went a little easier. When the smell came first, the thing to do was to give it a wide flank, come at it upwind, and get the story before moving on.

He was nearly even with the trees when he heard a cry, the small cry of a small thing, like a lamb, but it wasn't a lamb. It was a baby. He touched his spurs to Sandy and got to the trees on a lope.

Four buzzards lifted from the camp as Sandy settled to a halt and Sam slid from the saddle, fighting the heaves that pounded in his stomach. He yanked on the reins to keep the horse from backstepping, and then he looked at the camp.

It was a camp of Mexican folk who had come to the end of their luck. Two oxen slumped dead in the harness of a wooden-wheeled cart. Next to a mounded grave with a wooden cross lay the body of a man with its mouth open. Sam looked away. The baby's cry came again from the off side of the cart, where the last of the morning shade still lingered. Tugging on the reins, he stepped around the end of the cart. There was a young woman sitting blank-eyed against the wheel, rocking the baby vacantly. She didn't seem to have the strength or the focus to care for the baby beyond that automatic movement.

Sam knelt by the woman. *"¿Qué pasó?"* he asked. What happened?

She licked her lips. *"Muertos. Todos muertos."* Dead. All dead.

Sam nodded. *"Sí. Hombre muerto. Vacas muerto. Qué pasó?"* Yes. Dead man. Dead cows. What happened?

The woman rolled her eyes. *"Agua."* Water.

"¿Quiere agua?" You want water?

"No. No agua. Agua mala." No. No water. Bad water.

"¿Mala?" Bad?

"Veneno." Poison.

"¿Quiere agua? ¿Agua buena, fresca?" Do you want water? Good water? Fresh?

The woman nodded. Sam unslung one of his canteens and held it to her lips. She drank and nodded again. *"Gracias."*

He dribbled a little water on the baby's mouth, but the baby just sputtered and coughed and cried. Sam settled onto his heels, still squatting, and asked again what had happened.

The woman spoke rapidly in a voice somewhere between crying and heavy sighing, a voice full of agony and sadness, a voice that seemed far too old for a young mother. From her rambling, Sam pieced together the story. They had all drunk from a poisoned spring, all but the baby. Her husband and son had died first, and then her brother-in-law, who presumably had lived long enough to bury the other two in a common grave. The woman seemed certain that she, too, was going to die.

Sam offered her more water and she took

it, but it oozed out of her mouth and down her chin, sprinkling a few drops on the baby. She moved her mouth as if trying to speak, but no words came. Relaxing her hold on the baby to let it lie on her lap, she closed her eyes and leaned her head back against the hub of the wheel. She was on the way out, he could see that. He patted her hand and said the only thing he could think of, "*Vaya con Dios.*" God be with you. The hand fluttered, and that was it.

In less than an hour, Sam had buried the brother-in-law, cut loose the oxen, and, with Sandy straining, dragged the dead animals a hundred yards distant. All the while, the baby cried. When Sam returned to the cart, where he had stretched the woman out in the shade, the baby had crawled onto the mother's abdomen and was kneading at the dead left breast. That was the hardest moment, and it stayed with him through the burying, the mumbled words to God and the dead mother, and the long ride through daylight and darkness until he reached the town of Socorro.

La señora Ramos ground the dry oatmeal to a finer grain in her stone *metate* before cooking it for the baby. Fontaine sat at the table by candlelight, rolling a cigarette and then smoking it as the woman did her work.

When the gruel was cooked she set it aside to cool, then went about the task of changing the baby's diaper. Sam looked away, studying a crucifix that seemed to move on the wall as the candle flickered.

La señora Ramos spoke good English. "I cannot keep this baby, you know, not forever," she said as she spooned mush into the infant. She looked at Sam, and he nodded. "When I was younger and my house was full of children, I never counted them. Everybody's children went to everybody's house. What was one more? I had eight myself. And four dead ones." She crossed herself. Then she resumed feeding the baby. "But my children are gone now, to their own families, and I am an old widow. I have to wash clothes and clean houses. The time is past for me." She shook her head and then smiled as she looked into the baby's eyes.

Sam took out the makings and rolled another cigarette. He lit it with the candle and blew out a cloud of smoke. "What do you think we should do? Could we ask around and maybe find a home for it?"

She shrugged. "We could."

"You don't seem to like that idea."

"There are two problems. A family might take the baby in a sense of obligation. Or a family could get jealous who did not get the baby."

"Uh-huh." Fontaine ashed his cigarette in his palm and rubbed the ashes into his pant leg. "You must have another idea."

She raised her eyebrows. "We could offer the baby through the Church."

"What's the problem there?"

"There is a couple, the Reyes, who have money but no children."

"And you wouldn't want them to get the baby."

"I would not prefer it."

Sam looked at the ceiling and then back at the woman. He shook his head. "What do we do, then?"

"You could keep the baby. You found the baby and saved its life. It would not be wrong. Perhaps it is God's gift to you."

Sam nodded. The thought of keeping it had occurred to him as he had cradled the baby in his right arm on the long ride into Socorro. "I can think on it," he said. "But I don't know how I could take care of it. I've got to work, too."

La señora Ramos had apparently been doing some thinking herself. "Get yourself a young widow," she said.

Having told the señora he would think on

it, and having gotten her to agree to keep the baby for a week, Sam rode to Albuquerque with no more definite plan than to study on it.

Always before, when he had thought about marriage, Sam Fontaine had imagined a blue-eyed girl with light-colored hair, an innocent, untouched girl who, through his guidance, would step into adult life. There would be marriage and then children.

Now, life presented a different possible order. He had a child if he wanted it. The memory of the baby pushing against the dead mother's breast, together with the memory of it squirming against his own body as he cradled it on horseback, gave rise to a strong feeling he could not brush aside. Yes, he had a child if he wanted it, and he could find a marriage to match.

There was plenty to study in Albuquerque. He saw the blue-eyed girls, apparently untouched, and he saw their dark-eyed, dark-haired counterparts. He saw young mothers with their children, older mothers with older children, women without children but with the look of motherhood about them. As he studied, the girls moved him less and less, while the women interested him more and more. He did not covet these women, but in the mature presence of a woman who had had a child, there was a definite power or pull.

It was absurd to think of shopping for a woman as a man might look for a cow pony or a draft horse, but he did need to form a clear idea of what he was looking for. The señora, in her practical wisdom, had started him thinking that way. A young widow would not be rushed from girlhood into motherhood. She would have matured some, and she might already have a child or two. At any rate she would have her own baggage, as Sam would have his. There would be an equality of sorts. And a young widow, Sam thought for the first time, with a widening smile, would be fit to have more. That would be a nice mix, he thought — mine, hers, and ours.

The young widow began to take on a definite image. She was a woman, not a girl — a young mother with one or possibly two at her side. She had dark eyes, dark hair, and skin the color of dark honey. Working backwards, from child to marriage, had defined that for him — the baby should be raised in the language and customs of its original mother.

"Señora," he said, as he laid his hat on the table, "I have decided to keep the baby."

Then he winked. "But I have one question."

"Yes?"

"Is it a boy or a girl?"

La señora Ramos smiled. "He's a little boy. And we don't know his name, or whether he's been baptized, or —"

"Hold on," Sam interjected. "I've got to find the young widow first, and then we'll take care of the rest."

When he had sketched out the lines of his recent thinking, the señora nodded in agreement. "Well, we can look around," she said. "I know of one woman, in my town of Palomas."

"Down on the border?"

"Yes." At Sam's hesitation she added, "You could go take a look. You don't have to take the first one you see."

"It's a start," he said. Then, thinking, he asked, "What's the word for widow?"

"Viuda."

"Beeyutha."

"That's close."

"Will she be dressed in black?"

"I think he has more than one year dead."

"How do you say 'What does that mean?' "

"You'll need that one. *¿Qué quiere decir?*"

He practiced it a few times.

"And how do you say 'it doesn't matter'?"

"No le hace."

"Nolayossay."

"That's close. What doesn't matter?"

"Whether it was a boy or a girl. And there'll be other things." He thought for another minute and then said, "I think I'd feel funny ridin' down there and knockin' on her door."

"It would be her father's door. She lives at his house."

"All the more reason. Hmmm. Does she have children?"

"I think she has one girl."

"Do you think you could get her to come here for a visit? Do you know her that well?"

"I barely know her, but I know her family. I can try."

The young widow María and the niña Ramona came to Socorro for a stay. Mother and daughter were dark, darker than the niño (who still went by the name of Niño) or his late mother, darker than the dark honey of Sam's imagination. Not that the darkness mattered — *no le hace* — but he had to adjust the qualifications he had projected. He admired the woman's fine features and shapely body, but more than that, he felt readily comfortable with her presence. She seemed to take a liking to him —

probably would not have come if she had not been prepared to.

María was twenty-one and Sam was twenty-eight. Ramona was three and Niño was not yet a year old, the women agreed. María took a mother's interest in Niño, and Sam was instantly fond of Ramona, who, in turn, took a liking to both Sam and Sandy, as well as a natural interest in the baby. It looked to Sam as if everything was going to fit together.

After a month of round-robin acquaintance, Sam asked María to marry him, and she said *"Sí."*

They did not marry in the church or from her father's house, but with the justice of the peace in Socorro. Theirs was not a boisterous celebration, and María seemed pleased. That night, when she took him to her, she said, *"Te quiero mucho, Sem."*

He repeated the pledge in English. "I love you, María."

In the morning sunlight he sat on the edge of the bed and held her at arm's length, standing before him, his hands on her hips. It was a beautiful being he had joined himself with, this even-toned, full-bodied woman who in her presence meant togetherness and family. That was where it began, for them, the fitting together of a family, and now they could fill in with the daily confidences and agreements that had already begun to develop. He pulled her towards him and kissed her on the stomach. "My wife. *Mi mujer.*"

She held his head against her, the fingers of her left hand in his hair, the palm of her right hand against his cheek. *"Mi hombre."*

As the cool weather set in, Sam looked around for work to help them through the winter. There wasn't much work, but he did find two horses to break and train for plea-sure riding. He spent the afternoons at that, and so he brought in a few dollars in November.

One evening la señora Ramos came to visit. After the preliminaries she made it clear she had come with a purpose. She spoke in the pattern she had developed for speaking with María and Sam: first in Spanish, then backing up to repeat or clarify in English, as Sam's expressions made the need clear. And so she launched into this evening's business.

This was a beautiful thing, this life and this love between two people, the joining of a family, a full life for them all, a life of pride for Ramona and Roberto (as Niño had come to be called). Everybody could see it. But you know how people can be. Some people can have everything yet wish to have something that belonged to someone else. There was no need to tell names, but there was a couple in the town who thought that perhaps not enough care had been taken to discover Roberto's true family. These people thought perhaps Roberto's future had been determined too quickly, perhaps the matter needed reconsideration.

These people had spoken with the priest and with the judge, and it was hoped by this couple that Roberto might be placed with a family who had no interest in the matter, until a satisfactory inquiry could be made. It was thought that if Roberto proved to be indeed without a family, then he could be eligible for legal adoption, with lawyers and the court and all of that.

Sam and María sat side by side in their chairs, their hand grip growing tighter. But Roberto has a family, María said.

Yes, and nobody can deny that. But his place is not secure. It is clear that there are some people who want a baby enough to take it.

Sam and María looked at each other. He said, in broken Spanish, this is not a good town for us. There is not much work. I don't like to run, but this is not a good town for us.

I think you are right, resumed la señora Ramos. You do not have relatives here, or a business. You are my friends, and I do not like to see my friends leave, especially at my age, but I agree with you.

Sam took María's hand in both of his. We could go south, he said.

She shook her head, not violently, but to show there was no strain in that direction.

We could go north. To a place I saw on the cow trip. It is cold there, very cold in the winter.

At what distance does it lie? asked María.

In good weather, three weeks. In bad weather, who knows? Maybe not until spring.

Three weeks in good weather, said la señora Ramos. That seems to me to be a good place.

Sam looked at María. It is a good place, she said, even if it should be cold. What is it called?

Wyoming. On the other side of Colorado. Much wind and very cold. Nobody wants to go there. A good place.

They all laughed. It was seeming easier already.

Every night on the trip north, when they were bedded down in the wagon, María cried. Sometimes they made love when the children were asleep and sometimes they didn't, but every night she cried. Sam held her and hugged her and patted her, brushed the damp strands of hair from her face and kissed her. He came to understand that it was the distance from home, growing longer each day, that weighed on her. Even though her family seemed agreeable to letting her go from the very first, and even though she showed no strong desire to make a home near them, the separation was being felt sharply.

Sam wondered if it was anything else. Your friends?

No. My father and my mother.

Your country?

No. Just my parents.

Your brothers and your sisters?

Yes, them, too.

Sam took a skate on thin ice. Your dead husband?

No, no. My father and my mother.

"Te quiero mucho, María." I love you very much, María.

"Te quiero, Sem. Para siempre." I love you, Sam. Forever.

They rested a week in Denver and another four days in Cheyenne. It was an open winter so far, as folks said in Cheyenne. Trails were open north; trains were running east and west. There was plenty of time yet to get snowed in, but it was an open winter so far.

In mid-January the Fontaines filed on a quarter section of land, rolling plains country a few miles off the Platte. They rented a small house in town, a drafty clapboard shack that had been vacated by a Texas family who went back south for the weather. Sam and María patched cracks, kept a fire going in the sheet-iron stove, and waited for the thaw.

The family lived on deer meat all that winter. María, who was raised on tough beef, took to it fine, as did the children. Sam liked all food.

Will we be able to grow chiles here?

I think so. The summers are hot. They grow wheat. And I've seen apple trees.

This is good meat, but I will want to cook it with chiles.

We'll see. I think we can grow chiles.

María did not cry every night now, just once in a while. Things had come together again. For a while it had seemed as if they were four people, from different places, not living in any of them, speaking a mish-mash. Now it was seeming to flow together again, the ebb and flow of their common life, the melting of boundaries, the mingling of selves, the overflow and overlap of words. Sam could look back and hope that the worst was behind them, strung out in the cold trek north, left on the frozen plains, part of the wasteland between the place they left and the place they came to.

Spring came on slowly, starting in late March with the first green shoots of grass in the snowmelt, then freezing up solid again before the gradual teasing of warmer weather. In early May they took the wagon to their parcel, to camp out and get a view of things.

They set camp at a clump of chokecherry trees, where two draws came together. Sam and María spread a canvas for the children and then went to look at the greening branches.

A close look at the branches startled him. The branches were bristling with the furry green tips of leaves, and the smooth bark was freckled with white dots. The trees seemed to be bursting with life, eager for the new season.

"Una fruta," he said. A fruit.

"¿Buena?" Good?

"Sí. No muy dulce. Chica." Yes. Not very

sweet. Small. He pressed his left thumbnail against the tip of the little finger. *"Así de grande."* This big.

She nodded. *"Está bueno."* That's good.

They walked, hand in hand, to a rise in the ground where they could see their land slope away to the north.

"¿Te gusta?" he asked. It was important that she like the place.

"Sí, me gusta." Yes, I like it.

"¿Te gusta casa aquí?" You like the house here? He pointed down at the place where he thought to build a house.

"Sí."

Still, that night, she cried again, after they made love in the wagon.

Maybe it's the wagon, he thought.

In the morning she was sick, and when she returned from beyond the chokecherry trees, he looked up from the fire he was fanning with his hat. *"¿Estás enferma?"* Are you sick?

She took his hand, and he stood up.

"¿Qué pasa?" What's going on?

She looked at the wagon, where the children still slept. *"Estoy embarazada."*

He looked at her questioningly. *"¿Qué quiere decir?"* What does that mean?

She placed his hand on her stomach. *"Niño. Voy a tener un niño."* Child. I'm going to have a child.

Sam looked at his wife through watery eyes. *"¿Niño?"* Then his joy faded as he saw she was crying. *"¿Qué pasa?"*

"I sorry," she said. "I lie."

Her speaking in English alarmed him. She was confessing a lie and was coming over half-way to tell him. "Lie? *¿Mentira? ¿No niño?"*

"Sí, niño," she said, smiling through her tears.

"¿Qué mentira?" What lie?

She looked downward. *"Yo no era viuda."* I wasn't a widow.

"¿No viuda, tú?" No widow, you?

"No, no viuda." No, no widow.

"¿No esposo, no hombre? ¿No hombre muerto?" No husband, no man? No dead man?

"No, no esposo. Nunca." No, no husband. Never.

Sam smiled at her and kissed her on the forehead. He knelt and kissed her on the stomach, then stood up and held her hands as he looked her in the eyes. *"No le hace. No importa."* It doesn't matter. It's not important.

"¿Está bien?" It's all right?

"Sí. Tú eres mi mujer. Te quiero." Yes. You are my wife. I love you.

"Yo te quiero a ti, Sem. Para siempre. ¿Está bien, yo no viuda?" I love you, Sam. Forever. It's all right, I'm no widow?

"Está bien." It's all right. He loosened his right hand and made a triangular, circular motion to take in her, the baby that would be, and himself. Then he made a wider motion to take in themselves and the two children sleeping in the wagon. *"Familia."*

"Sí. Familia."

TRAILS END

The sun overhead looked as if it hadn't moved for two hours. It just hung there, hot enough to melt hell's hinges. My horse was still walking, but it had been a day and a half since we'd had water, and his eyes were starting to roll. I said, half to myself and half to my horse, "We'll be gettin' to water soon. It's not time to stand in line for a harp yet." I knew that on the other side of those buttes there was a little dirty town known as Five Pigs, and even though it didn't have much, it had water.

Dusting down the main drag of Five Pigs, looking slanchways out from under my hat brim, I saw townsfolk lounging in the doorways. They didn't like my looks, I could tell, but they didn't have no corner on that market. And I couldn't say as I blamed them. At the horse trough in front of the livery stable I let my horse drink about a gallon or so, then pulled him back so's he wouldn't waterlog himself. After I tied him to the hitching rail, I plunged my own head into the trough. It felt good. Pivoting on my heel, I picked my sombie off the saddle horn, loosed the thong on my Colt, and headed for the watering hole known, according to the shingle that passed for a sign, as the Silver Gila. A sawed-off little jasper no cleaner than myself, leaning against the wall of the general store, spoke up.

"You ought not to be so stingy with your hoss on a hot day like today, stranger."

By now my mouth was wet enough to afford the luxury of a spit, so I did. Not at him, but into the dust off the side of the sidewalk. "Was I you," I said, "I'd mind my own. If I want any talk out of you, I'll slap it out." I raked him with a scowl that I thought might keep him for a while, then clunked along the board sidewalk and pushed myself through the batwings of the Silver Gila.

"Whatcha need, stranger?" the barkeep asked, as he polished a glass with what he must have called an apron. Looked to me like he was getting the glass greasier as he went along.

"Three fingers Red-Eye," I said.

I took in the crowd in the saloon as I tossed down the whiskey. This was a hard-case bunch, I could tell that. The drought wasn't making any of them any richer, and if I ever saw the fear of sheep in cattlemen's faces, I saw it then. Not that they took me for a sheepherder, but maybe for a sheepman's hired gun. I wasn't anybody's hired gun, but I thought these fellas might want to push me around, one way or the other. I decided to keep them on the run before they tried to buffalo me.

I cleared my throat and shot an oyster into the spittoon. "Barkeep!"

"Yeah, what now?"

"More whiskey!"

With his left hand he skidded the full bottle down the bar to me. "Just remember to pay before you pass out," he said. He kept his right hand below the bar — on a double-barrelled Greener, I figured.

"Barkeep!" I put more bite into it this time.

"What the hell you want now?"

"Two of your cigars." With his left hand he pulled two out of his shirt pocket and tossed them on the bar.

"Need a match?" he sneered.

"Nope, just company." By now I had picked out the guy I figured was the town's Billy Bad-Ass. He was standing hipshot at the bar, wearing a tall Stetson pushed back and a Colt tied way down on his leg. "You," I said, "shag your ass over here and have a drink and a smoke with me."

His hand hung right over the grip of his

Colt. "Yeah," he said, "and who might I be obliged to for such hospitality?"

"Deke Maginnis," I said, and that did it. The chatter stopped dead, the poker chips quit rattling, and everybody froze. "Don't let a name scare you," I said. I bit off the end of one cigar, spit it onto the sawdust floor, licked the cigar, and lit it. By now the big galoot had joined me.

"Sorry I didn't recognize you, Mr. Maginnis," he said. "Of course I'll have a drink and a smoke with you, and be obliged."

"That's good," I said, curling my lip at the rest of the crowd. "A man likes a little sociable company after he's crossed over the country I just crossed. Never seed so many dead steers in one year."

"And it's a damn bloody shame," he said. He dropped a shot of whiskey into his neck, and set his jaw grim. "These damn woolly lovers have sheeped us off the upper range, and now they're crowding us off the waterholes. Next thing you know, there won't be such a thing as free range in this territory. The way the cattle are ganted up and dropping off like flies, it'll be a wonder if any of the little ranchers make it through this year."

"The hell you say," I said, taking the crowd at a glance. I picked up a quarter and tossed it at a peach-faced lad barely big enough to fill up a Stetson. "Here, Sonny," I said, "you go out to the hitching rail in front of the livery stable, and you take my steeldust gelding, and you let him drink about a gallon and a half or maybe two gallons of water, and you tie him back up. Anyone puts in his two bits worth, you tell him to send the bill to Deke Maginnis."

"Yes, sir," he chirped back, and hustled out through the batwings.

"And you," I said to my new *compadre*, "what's your handle?"

"I'm Niles Nelson," he said, "and mighty pleased to make your acquaintance, Mr. Maginnis. Seems to me you might be the best thing that's happened to this town in a while." He looked around to the other ranchers in the crowd, and they all grumbled yeah's and I-think-so's and you-betcha's. I took the lead from there.

"If you don't mind my saying so, Mr. Nelson, the whole lot of you look like you've looked at your hole card and it wasn't pretty."

"I don't mind a man speaking the truth, Mr. Maginnis. The fact is, these four-flushin' sheepherders have got us with our backs to the wall."

"Yeah," broke in another, "they got us between a rock and a hard spot." The crowd in back started grumbling again.

"Well," said I, and they quieted, "it looked to me, as I came across this country on the way in, that they've done sheeped out the upper grassland along the Little Sisters range, and they're takin' over the Gila Flats. Next thing, they'll have you pushed up against Buitre Pass, and on the other side of that there's nothing but broken country, all rocks and sand, with no more grass than a jackrabbit could live on."

"You hit it dead center, Mister," said one grizzled old coot.

"Well," I said, "seems to me you fellas got to get organized. You can't let those sheep lovers run roughshod over you and ruin the range. Come a good year, and good rain, this range'll be fit for grazin' again, 'less you let them over-graze it."

Nelson took over again. "That's just what we've been talkin' about, Mr. Maginnis. And what we need is someone to pull us together. Someone to ramrod us so we can push back!"

"You look like a man cut out for it," I said dryly.

"Me, no sir. I can hit a silver dollar at fifty paces, and I can fork my own broncs, but I'm no leader. We need a leader, someone we can look up to — someone that'll strike fear into the hearts of those stinkin' sheeptenders."

At this point the whole saloon was rumbling with yeah, you betcha, you damn right, and so forth. I thought to myself, they think I'm the Texas Gun. I dropped another shot down my gullet, winced, and regarded Nelson narrowly. "What's your bargain, Nelson? I know you're not just talkin' to pass the time of day. Let's palaver."

"I think I speak for the Cattlemen's Association of Five Pigs," he said, looking around to the crowd. They all muttered that he did. "We'd like to offer you ten percent of each of our herds, come fall roundup, in return for your getting us back our waterholes and our range."

"That sounds mighty temptin'," I said, "but I got no hankerin' to go out and shoot a bunch of sheep. Next thing you know, you got to shoot a few sheepherders, and then someone's got to bury 'em. Don't know as that's my line of work."

"Mr. Maginnis," Nelson resumed, "you do the work you see fit to do, and the rest of us will look after the cleaning up. Ten percent?" He stuck out his hand, and I shook it.

Next day, the Silver Gila was fuller than before, and I'd guess every rancher in the territory — exceptin' sheepmen — was at the meeting. When everybody had wet his whistle and got his sap flowin' I banged on the bar with my hogleg and called the meeting to order. "You gents," I hollered out, "have asked me to take the lead, and I've agreed to do it. But I have to know, before I take another step, if I have your complete support."

There was a long and loud rumble of damn-betcha and hell-yes.

"And I want you to know that we can't pull this thing through without personal sacrifice on the part of each and every one of you. And I don't mean lives. Every one of us can come through this fight alive, if we move right. But you're gonna have to be willin' to give up a little of what you've worked so hard to earn."

"We've already done that by offering you ten percent," one ranny shouted out.

"I'm talkin' about more than that," I said, "and not for me, neither. I mean sacrifice." That held them for a minute, and I rolled a quirly and lit it. I shot out a cloud of smoke, then addressed them again. "You men still with me?"

There was a louder rumble than ever before. These men wanted to stop the tide of sheep.

"All right. Each of you go back to your spread and sit tight until you hear from me. Stay away from lighted windows, and don't ride the range except you go two or three strong. And don't shoot no sheep until the party starts. You'll be hearin' from me. Meetin's adjourned."

Nelson came up to me as the cattlemen dispersed, and he poured me a drink. "By the lord Harry," he said, "I think we've got more group spirit than we've ever had before. What do you have figured for your first move, Mr. Maginnis?"

"Tomorrow, come good daylight, you and me, Mr. Nelson, we ride."

The sun was burning the nipples of the Little Sisters when Nelson and I rattled our hocks out of Five Pigs. "Your canteen full?" I asked.

"You bet."

"Your Winchester loaded?"

"Yep."

"Good. You might need both before this day's through."

"I know you've got a plan, Mr. Maginnis, but could you give me an idea what it is?"

"My think-box don't work like most men's," I said.

"That's why we wanted you," he said, quickly.

"This here's a plan that some men won't like."

"You're the leader."

"You remember what I said yesterday about sacrifice?"

"Sure I do."

"Well, today's the day we jump into it, with both boots."

First ranch we rode into was the Vaca Flaca. We reined up and called out to the owner, one Ben Whitley. He came bowleggin' out of the ranchhouse like the whorehouse was caught on fire. "Well, Maginnis," he said, "are we ready to move?"

"Yep," I said, "and we start right here. Whitley, I want you or one of your hands to set fire to your house and barn and sheds, and pull over your windmill, and then all of you ride with us."

"What?! Burn my headquarters?"

"It's either burn your headquarters or lose your hindquarters," I said. "If we want to stop those sheep, we got to burn off the range so they won't have anything to push forward to."

"What about my cattle? What will they do for feed and water?"

"When we get those stinkin' sheepherders

pushed back over the other side of the Little Sisters, you'll have good grass and water, and plenty of it."

"I sure hope you know what you're doing!"

"You voted for me, didn't you?"

"Yeah, I did."

By noontime the range was covered by a thick black smoke as the withered grass went skyward in a million wisps. By then we had burned a dozen ranch headquarters, and we were over sixty strong. The range we rode over was hotter than a blacksmith's apron, and every man jack of us had a handkerchief tied over his nose and mouth to keep out the black particles that filled the air. Nelson pulled his cayuse alongside mine as we headed for the biggest ranch, the Rolling Willow. "Maginnis," he shouted, "how much of this we got left to do?"

"We gotta burn the whole range," I hollered back, "the whole length of Gila Flat, to keep them from coming any farther."

"Then what?"

"Then we start pushing."

"Back across the Little Sisters?"

"That's the only way." I spurred my horse onward, to see if we could get out of this cloud of smoke and catch a breather at the Rolling Willow before we set a torch to it.

I knew that Jack Kenton, the barrel-chested, two-fisted owner of the Rolling Willow, would not like what I had in store. He met us at the gate, Winchester in the crook of his arm. "What the hell you men think you're up to?"

"We're fightin' fire with fire," I said, leaning with both hands on the pommel of my saddle. "We're burning a swath of no-man's land between the sheep and the rest of this valley. It's the only way to stop them at this point, to give them nothing to push ahead for."

"What do you think you're gonna do here?"

"Think, hell," I snorted, "I know. Just what we did at the other places. These men," I said, with a sweep of the arm, "have made their sacrifice, and they're here to see that you make yours." He took one look at the rest of them, every one of them grimy with soot, sweaty from hard riding, and grim-set from their work.

"All right," he said, "but let me get a few things out of my ranch house."

"Make it quick," I said, "we're traveling light." Two punchers rode forward and roped the support posts of his windmill, and a couple more started setting fire to his hayloft. These men were taking to their work with enthusiasm. Smoke was billowing out of the barn when Kenton came rushing out of his house, stuffing deeds and portraits into a flour sack. "Now we ride," I commanded, and we were off again, stronger by a dozen men.

Back in Five Pigs, the town itself was filmed in a light coat of ash. The hitching racks were lined with cow ponies standing hipshot. The saloons were filled — there couldn't have been a cowpoke on the range. What cows hadn't been caught in the grassfire had been pushed up against Buitre Pass, with no water and feed. The ranchers had gathered in Five Pigs to wait for my next move.

In the Silver Gila, I commanded a poker table and a bottle of Red-Eye. I hadn't had to pay for a drink since my first one in this town, and I was getting to like it. I put my spurred and booted foot up on the poker table, and I slugged down a shot of whiskey. "Boys," I said to the men within hearing distance — and the sidewalk was crowded outside as well — "Boys, we struck a mighty good blow today. I'd say we drew first blood. And I'm proud of each and every one of you for putting the common good before your personal needs and wants. Each of you has done his part in stopping that dirty grey blanket of sheep from coming any farther. Come sundown tomorrow, we'll have pushed those smelly woollies on t'other side of the Little Sisters. Then we push the cattle back across the burned range to the grass and water on Gila Flat. This basin will be ours again, and any snivellin' sheep-man will think twice before he crosses the Little Sisters again. For right now," I said, hoisting my drink aloft, "we drink to the campaign!" The silence broke and a rumble followed. These men had gambled, and the winners' stakes were now within their grasp. I could tell they knew it, what with the scattered oaths and curses that rippled through the crowd. Any sheepmen who were around come sunup would be in a bad way, after all that these cowmen had lost.

I was just putting my other foot up on the poker table when a long-legged hombre pushed his way through the batwings and up to the bar. He looked familiar, but I couldn't place him. "What the hell kind of barbecue you men having in this country, anyways?" he asked, clinking his coin.

He being a stranger, no one answered. It was up to me, I guessed.

"Laredo," I called out to the barkeep (that was his name, I'd learned), "give this man a cigar. Come over here and have a drink, stranger, and tell me what you rode through today, and from where."

He downed a shot of my whiskey and wiped his upper lip with his lower. "I come over from Cinco Piedras today, through the Little Sisters." That quieted the crowd, for we all wanted to know how the sheepherders had taken in the burn job we'd done.

"Well," I said, "here's how." And I tipped back my drink, and then filled us both up again. "Tell me, stranger, how did them oily woolly-chasers seem to be actin'?"

"Oh, I met them t'other side of the Little Sisters. They didn't seem to be too worried, just glad to get back over on t'other side."

"We scared them that quick, eh?"

"Don't reckon they were that scared."

"What you mean by that?"

"Seems they'd sheeped out all the grass on Gila Flat, and dried up the water holes, to where they couldn't have kept but a few hundred head of sheep anyway, so they pulled their freight yesterday. Said the cows could have what was left. They'd come back next year. Me, not caring all that much for woollies, but not looking for any more trouble than naturally came my way, I just pushed on. They were right about the grass and water — Gila Flat's about as smooth and dry as a lizard's belly."

The saloon was quiet as a morgue, and everyone was looking at me. "The hell you say." The words came quickly to me.

"The hell I do say. And by the way, what was all the burnin' down here in the valley?"

"You ask a lot of questions for a man who hasn't even told us who he is," I said, not exactly pleased by the turn things had taken.

"Name's Deke Maginnis, if it's anything to you," he said. He poured himself a whiskey with his left hand, keeping his right to linger above his pistol butt. "What's yours?" He smiled like he knew the answer, and my hole card never looked poorer than it did at that moment. He bit off the end of his cigar, licked it, and lit it, while he waited for an answer.

Nelson broke the silence. "See here, stranger, this man here is Deke Maginnis, as he himself told us, and just today he led us on a campaign to burn out those scrubby sheep!" As he spoke the words, the truth seemed to crawl over him. He looked sharply at me. By now I had taken both boots off the table and set down my whiskey glass. The crowd had moved in tight as a whore's corset, and I was worried. Nelson turned to the newcomer. "Tell me, then, who you think this man sitting here is."

This was the part I was not destined to enjoy.

"That man sitting there?" He started to laugh. "That's Las Cruces Charlie! He's been run out of every town in the territory — Tucson, Nogales, Tombstone, you name it." Then he curled his lip, rested his hand on his pistol, and looked around at the crowd. "And don't nobody lay a hand on him till I'm through with him." His steely gaze rested on me. "Get up and follow me."

I did.

He cut a wide swath to the batwings and escorted me to the hitchrack, with two hundred pair of eyes on me. "You, Charlie, you went by my name? That's a laugh! A real horse laugh! And you know what? I like a good joke, a joke like the one you pulled here. And you know what else? I'm gonna give you a twenty-minute head start on the honest ranchers of Five Pigs."

I just stood there, hornswoggled. He wasn't going to do what Deke Maginnis was famous for doing. I'd heard some ugly stories about him, like the rest of the town had — dragging Mexicans around, shooting the queues off Chinamen.

"You better fork your hoss and get moving, Charlie." He pulled out his watch, held it in his left hand, and laid his right hand on his widow-maker. "I'll hold 'em for twenty minutes. Recommend you go by way of the Little Sisters."

So there I was, riding hell-for-leather across the scorched range, through what looked like a battlefield littered with burned and swollen cattle, toppled windmills, the charred remains of ranch houses and barns, and drifting flecks of ash everywhere. My horse was wheezing, and my nostrils were filled with the stuff, even with my kerchief up. The air cleared a mite as we pushed across Gila Flat, and below me I could see the honest ranchers, as Deke Maginnis called them, coming out of the burned plains and pounding after me. Thought I to myself, I'd have to be on my toes when I crossed trails with those sheepherders.

Then I was at the foot of the Little Sisters, and my horse was starting to get winded. I got off and walked him for a ways, and I looked back to see the ranchers gaining ground on me. I put a foot in the stirrup, and as I swung my leg over the cantle, I told myself for the first time in two days, I sure have a knack for making a mess wherever I go. Then I thought of Deke Maginnis, and how hard he must be laughing back in the Silver Gila, and I smiled to think how nice it was to bring a little sunshine into the life of at least one fellow human.

About the Author

John D. Nesbitt lives in the plains country of Wyoming, and he teaches English and Spanish at Eastern Wyoming College in Torrington. His Western stories and modern West stories have appeared in many magazines and anthologies. Three Western novels, *One-Eyed Cowboy Wild*, *Twin Rivers*, and *Wild Rose of Ruby Canyon*, have been published by Walker and Company. He also has three collections of short stories: *One Foot in the Stirrup: Western Stories*, *I'll Tell You What: Fiction With Voice*, and *Antelope Sky: Stories of the Modern West*. His fiction, nonfiction, book reviews, and poetry have been widely published. He has won many prizes and awards for his work, including a Wyoming Arts Council literary fellowship for his fiction writing.

The employees of Thorndike Press hope you have enjoyed this Large Print book. All our Large Print titles are designed for easy reading, and all our books are made to last. Other Thorndike Press Large Print books are available at your library, through selected bookstores, or directly from us.

For information about titles, please call:

(800) 223-2336

To share your comments, please write:

Publisher
Thorndike Press
P.O. Box 159
Thorndike, Maine 04986